PRAISE FOR DONNA GRANT'S
BEST-SELLING ROMANCE NOVELS

"A breathtaking tale...I absolutely loved it!"
  —Romance Junkies on Dark Craving, Dark Kings Series

"The author has created a fantastic and mesmerizing fantasy world with intriguing twists, surprises and unique elements that keeps the reader turning the pages to the very end."
  —Night Owl Reviews on Dark Heat, Dark Kings Series

"Evie and Malcolm is a couple that makes it impossible not to love them."
  —The Jeep Diva, Dark Warriors Series

"Grant's smoldering seventh Dark Warrior outing will grip readers from the first page, immersing them in her wounded, lonely couple's journey of redemption...each scene is filled with Grant's clever, complex characters and trademark sizzle."
  —Romantic Times Magazine (RT Book Reviews), Dark Warriors Series

DON'T MISS THESE OTHER SPELLBINDING NOVELS

BY NYT & USA TODAY BESTSELLING AUTHOR DONNA GRANT

~

CONTEMPORARY PARANORMAL

DRAGON KINGS SERIES

(Spin off series from **DARK KINGS SERIES)**

Book 1: Dragon Revealed (novella)

Book 2: Dragon Mine

~

REAPER SERIES

Book 1: Dark Alpha's Claim

Book 2: Dark Alpha's Embrace

Book 3: Dark Alpha's Demand

Books 1-3 Bundle: Tall Dark Deadly Alpha

Book 4: Dark Alpha's Lover

Book 5: Dark Alpha's Night

Book 6: Dark Alpha's Hunger

Book 7: Dark Alpha's Awakening

Book 8: Dark Alpha's Redemption

Book 9: Dark Alpha's Temptation

Book 10: Dark Alpha's Caress

Book 11: Dark Alpha's Obsession

Book 12: Dark Alpha's Need

~

DARK KINGS SERIES

Book 15: Ignite

Book 16: Fever

Book 16.5: Dragon Lost (novella)

Book 17: Flame

Book 18: Inferno

The Dragon King Coloring Book

Dragon King Special Edition Character Coloring Book: Rhi

Book 19: Whisky and Wishes, A Dark Kings Special Holiday Novella

Book 20: Heart of Gold, A Dark Kings Special Valentine's Novella

Book 21: Of Fire and Flame

DARK WARRIORS SERIES

Book 1: Midnight's Master

Book 2: Midnight's Lover

Book 3: Midnight's Seduction

Book 4: Midnight's Warrior

Book 5: Midnight's Kiss

Book 6: Midnight's Captive

Book 7: Midnight's Temptation

Book 8: Midnight's Promise

Book 8.5: Midnight's Surrender (novella)

CHIASSON SERIES

Book 1: Wild Fever

Book 2: Wild Dream

Book 3: Wild Need

Book 4: Wild Flame

Book 5: Wild Rapture

~

LARUE SERIES

Book 1: Moon Kissed

Book 2: Moon Thrall

Book 3: Moon Struck

Book 4: Moon Bound

~

WICKED TREASURES

Book 1: Seized by Passion

Book 2: Enticed by Ecstasy

Book 3: Captured by Desire

Books 1-3: Wicked Treasures Box Set

~

HISTORICAL PARANORMAL

THE KINDRED SERIES

Book 0.5: Everkin (short story)

Book 1: Eversong

Book 2: Everwylde

Book 3: Everbound

Book 4: Evernight

Book 5: Everspell

~

DARK SWORD SERIES

Book 1: Dangerous Highlander

Book 2: Forbidden Highlander

Book 3: Wicked Highlander

Book 4: Untamed Highlander

Book 5: Shadow Highlander

Book 6: Darkest Highlander

ROGUES OF SCOTLAND SERIES

Book 1: The Craving

Book 2: The Hunger

Book 3: The Tempted

Book 4: The Seduced

Books 1-4: Rogues of Scotland Box Set

THE SHIELDS SERIES

Book 1: A Dark Guardian

Book 2: A Kind of Magic

Book 3: A Dark Seduction

Book 4: A Forbidden Temptation

Book 5: A Warrior's Heart

Mystic Trinity (a series connecting novel)

DRUIDS GLEN SERIES

Book 1: Highland Mist

Book 2: Highland Nights

Book 3: Highland Dawn

Book 4: Highland Fires

Book 5: Highland Magic

Mystic Trinity (a series connecting novel)

~

SISTERS OF MAGIC TRILOGY

Book 1: Shadow Magic

Book 2: Echoes of Magic

Book 3: Dangerous Magic

Books 1-3: Sisters of Magic Box Set

~

THE ROYAL CHRONICLES NOVELLA SERIES

Book 1: Prince of Desire

Book 2: Prince of Seduction

Book 3: Prince of Love

Book 4: Prince of Passion

Books 1-4: The Royal Chronicles Box Set

Mystic Trinity (a series connecting novel)

~

MILITARY ROMANCE / ROMANTIC SUSPENSE

SONS OF TEXAS SERIES

Book 1: The Hero

Book 2: The Protector

Book 3: The Legend

Book 4: The Defender

Book 5: The Guardian

COWBOY / CONTEMPORARY

HEART OF TEXAS SERIES

Book 1: The Christmas Cowboy Hero

Book 2: Cowboy, Cross My Heart

Book 3: My Favorite Cowboy

Book 4: A Cowboy Like You

Book 5: Looking for a Cowboy

Book 6: A Cowboy Kind of Love

STAND ALONE BOOKS

Home for a Cowboy Christmas

Mutual Desire

Forever Mine

Savage Moon

Dark Beginnings: A First in Series Boxset

Contains:

Chiasson Series, Book 1: Wild Fever

LaRue Series, Book 1: Moon Kissed

The Royal Chronicles Series, Book 1: Prince of Desire

Check out Donna Grant's Online Store for autographed books, character themed goodies, and more at www.DonnaGrant.com/shop

DARK ALPHA'S OBSESSION

REAPERS, BOOK 11

DONNA GRANT

DARK ALPHA'S OBSESSION
© 2021 by DL Grant, LLC
Cover Design © 2021 by Charity Hendry
Formatting © 2021 by Charity Hendry

Excerpt from: **DRAGON MINE**
© 2021 by DL Grant, LLC

ISBN 13: 978-1942017813
Available in ebook, audio, and print editions.
All rights reserved.

www.DonnaGrant.com
www.MotherofDragonsBooks.com

CHAPTER ONE

Achill Island, Ireland
End of July

Tonight was the same as countless others. Same captivating speech by her brother. Same engrossed faces, watching him with a mixture of awe and reverence. Same security in place, ensuring that the star —her sibling—was safe.

But something was off.

Fianna methodically scanned the faces in the room, looking for anything that might tell her who was responsible. But no matter how hard she looked, she couldn't find it. No one appeared out of place. Then again, few rarely did during the first meetings. Because that's what this was. The first of three gatherings before Dorcha chose who would be welcomed into their organization.

She remained in the shadows, inspecting each face of the thirty gathered to put them to memory. It was her duty to spot trouble. And she was damned good at it. While her brother had a silver tongue that could enrapture a room with just a few words, her skills ran to battle, weapons, and magic. She detested being the center of attention and was quite happy fading into the background.

Movement out of the corner of her eye caught her attention. She turned her head and spotted her brother as he made his way to the makeshift stage that had been erected just for him in the ballroom. Their gazes briefly met. Dorcha shot her a wink before he put a huge smile on his face and waved to the gathered crowd.

She had no idea how he did this night after night. He thrived on it, while the very thought of repeating the speeches made her want to gouge her eyes out. Then again, Dorcha didn't understand why she loved to train daily or got such a thrill from maintaining his security. They were, as their father often said, as different as night and day.

Fianna looked to the door and saw latecomers entering just as her brother's voice filled the room. She paid no attention to Dorcha. Her job was to keep an eye on those who attended in case anyone made an attempt on her sibling's life. Few truly understood how important Dorcha was.

But they would soon enough. Everyone always did.

The entirety of her and Dorcha's lives had led up to what was about to come to fruition. Fianna had trained tirelessly, became proficient at ancient magic that had been forgotten, and learned to fight with a unique set of weapons. While Dorcha had absorbed knowledge from archaic scrolls and perfected his speaking voice.

Fianna waited until the door had closed behind the last individual before she made her way around the perimeter of the room. Their meeting place was none other than Moorehall. It had a striking edifice with dark gray stone set against the vibrant, verdant surroundings. At times, she gazed upon the splendor of the manor and felt sorry that humans couldn't witness such breathtaking grandeur. Thanks to Fae magic, the mortals believed the manor was haunted and nothing but a crumbling house that had been neglected and forgotten.

Fianna moved slowly, keeping far from the guests. Her security team was set up throughout the house. Some were stationed purposefully to be seen, while others were hidden so as not to draw attention to themselves.

Once she made it to the other side of the stage, she set up in her customary position and continued scrutinizing those gathered. With her brother's voice droning on in the background, she noticed that most laughed at his jokes, nodded their heads in agreement, or clapped with enthusiasm at his comments. But not everyone. Her attention locked on the three who did none of those things.

Two males stood at the back with their arms crossed over their chests and looks of discontent on their faces. Their heads were tilted towards each other as they spoke in whispers, alerting her that they had most likely come together. She nodded to two guards nearest the pair and jerked her chin to the men. Her people had stationed themselves to intervene should it become necessary.

And a couple of times, it had been necessary.

People didn't always like what Dorcha had to say. But it needed to be said, and if he were the only one strong and brave enough to say it, then it fell to him. Fianna would be there to make sure no harm came to him. He had a great destiny ahead of him—a calling that would change the Fae forever.

Her gaze slid to the other guest, who made no motion of agreement in reaction to her brother's words. The male stood tall, his gaze steady as he observed Dorcha. Fianna leaned to the side to get a better view of him. He wore a black leather racing jacket over a solid gray tee, which prohibited her from seeing more of his physique other than his broad shoulders. His thick, black hair was trimmed short, the kind of cut a male wore when he didn't want to be bothered with styling his hair. He had a strong, clean jawline, a regal nose, and full and utterly sexy lips.

Handsome? He was definitely that. But there was something else about him. An air of danger, maybe? The fact that she couldn't figure him out as she did others intrigued her. Perhaps a little too much because she could never turn away from a puzzle. And he was, without a doubt, a mystery.

He shifted slightly, taking in a deep breath that lifted his shoulders as he stuffed his fingers into the front pockets of his jeans. She noticed his gaze moving about as if he were sizing up those around him. Fianna was instantly on alert. The first meetings brought in all sorts of Fae, and the larger crowds made her extra vigilant. However, she had to remind herself that this gathering was one that led to something special—as all first meetings did. Perhaps this male suspected that and was looking out for himself.

Her stomach fluttered when the Fae's lips suddenly turned up slightly at the corners, transforming his handsome face into something...breathtaking. Fianna instinctively took a step back. She wanted to run to her room and put as much distance between herself and the male as she could. Forget every second since she had laid eyes on him. But that wasn't an option for her. Not now, at least.

She forced herself to hold her ground and look anywhere but at his face. Little by little, she gained control of her suddenly erratic and foolish emotions. It had been a long time since she had been so...overcome. She was grateful that neither Dorcha nor her father had witnessed the episode. Yet even when she had control of herself, she didn't dare look at the Fae again. That would be idiotic, and she was anything but.

Well, most days anyway.

One of the female guards took a half-step forward from her position, drawing Fianna's gaze. Fianna followed the guard's line of sight and saw what had gotten her attention. One of the guests had noticed that the male she had been ogling—or rather, *watching*—hadn't been smiling or clapping. The guest's growing frown alerted Fianna that he was about to take action. She snapped her gaze to the guard nearest the male and gave a nod.

Dorcha's meetings had a way of exciting most in the room to his cause. And, sometimes, they took it as an insult when others didn't display the same sort of enthusiasm. Fianna had trained her people well. There was no need to tell them what to do as they observed everything. They all noticed what was going on and simply waited for her to give the cue.

Fianna watched as the guard came up alongside the riled guest and said a few words in his ear. The Fae instantly calmed and returned to his position. And, just like that, the situation was defused.

Unable to help herself, Fianna's gaze swung back to the Fae who had caused such a stir in both the other guest and her. Only to find his eyes locked on her. Her lungs seized, her heart skipped a beat, and the very air became charged with surprise—and curiosity. She was hidden. And yet, this Fae had somehow located her. She was captivated. That, in combination with her reaction to him, was a sign that she should stay far, far away from him.

The Fae bowed his head to her as he went back to listening to Dorcha. But Fianna wasn't fooled. He had been good enough to detect her, which meant he was skilled. The kind of skill that few possessed. The kind she trained every day to achieve. Someone of his talents would be a great addition to the security team. And when it came to her brother's safety, she was willing to sacrifice just about anything.

But if she brought the Fae onto her team, she knew what would happen. As much as she loved Dorcha and wanted him to succeed, Fianna wouldn't go down that path. She had been pulled back from it once already. It was a miracle she was even standing there today. She wasn't about to test herself again.

Hopefully, the stranger would leave this meeting and not return for the second. If he did, she doubted he would come for the third. Though there was a chance that he would. And if that happened, and Dorcha allowed him into their organization, she would have to face things head-on. Until then, she would continue as if nothing had happened.

And keep everything to herself.

Fianna was glad that her father wasn't here tonight. He always seemed to know when she battled the demons within. So many times, she had tried to lie to him. And every time, he had known. At least this once, she would be able to keep her secret. Dorcha and her father were the only two who knew what Fianna battled. It was a secret that would never be leaked because their family name had suffered enough, and her da wouldn't let that happen again.

The fact that she could get control of herself before things got out of hand proved how far she had come. She would not succumb. No matter how often her father warned her that she wasn't strong enough. She would prove him wrong. He and Dorcha were all Fianna had in the world, and she wouldn't do anything to disappoint either of them. The simple fact that they continued to stand by her told her how much they loved her.

Fianna forced herself to look around the room. She prayed for something else to focus on, but the crowd was quiet and calm. At any other time, she would be happy with such an outcome. But right now, she needed a distraction from the turmoil within.

She believed that she had gotten past the old ways that had nearly taken her down a dark path forever—lost to her family and herself. It seemed so long ago. Like another lifetime, really. She had become complacent, content. And look what that had gotten her. She hated this…*thing*…inside her that tried to rule her. She did everything right, followed all the guidelines. Why had it chosen her?

More importantly, why couldn't she vanquish it once and for all?

She swallowed past the lump of emotion in her throat as she grasped that she might never be free of such a burden—no matter how hard she trained, no matter how accomplished a warrior she was. It made her wonder why her father and Dorcha allowed her to remain with them. She knew that if anything got out about her affliction, it could—and *would*—ruin everything her father had been working towards all these thousands of years. He had lost so much, given up so much. He, above anyone else, deserved to achieve that which he desired most.

Just thinking of her father and how he had stood beside her gave Fianna the strength she needed to stand tall. He was the one she had leaned on during her lowest time. He was the one who'd made her face the demons, who told her that only the strongest of their line survived. He had never told her that he would disown her if she didn't get herself straight, but he hadn't needed to. It had been unspoken and had been what'd propelled Fianna to prove that she was worthy of his approval. Despite the tremendous uphill battle, Fianna had gotten herself together and had made her father proud.

And that day had altered her life irrevocably. It was what kept her motivated now, kept her focused.

"Thank you," Dorcha said.

Her brother's words pulled her from her thoughts, alerting her that the speech was finished. Fianna swallowed and nodded to her guards as the room erupted into applause and cheers. She was surprised to find even the handsome Fae clapping, albeit not as enthusiastically as some others. He didn't look her way again, and she was thankful for that.

Dorcha smiled, nodding to those in attendance as the applause continued. He raised his hands for quiet. Once the room fell silent, he said, "I hope you liked what you heard tonight. If so, return tomorrow night for more. See you then!"

The minute the words were out of his mouth, Dorcha was off the stage. Fianna remained behind with the other guards to ensure that no one tried to follow her brother or linger in the hopes of getting another glimpse. She found herself searching the crowd for the handsome Fae, but he was gone. She let out a sigh of relief, even as she felt a slight pang in her heart.

But she would ignore that part. Because she'd escaped something that had the potential to destroy everything.

CHAPTER TWO

It was one thing for Rordan to take on the task of spy. It was quite another to infiltrate a group of Fae who were hellbent on continuing the Others. The very thought made him want to hit something.

The Others had begun with a Druid from another realm, Moreann, who had sought to claim Earth as hers because her planet's magic was dying. Moreann hadn't cared that the Dragon Kings ruled this realm. She'd devised a plan that she believed would be the Kings' downfall and would allow her and her people to rule on Earth.

As powerful as the Druid was, it wasn't enough. Moreann

enlisted the aid of the Light Queen, Usaeil. However, even the two of them together didn't have sufficient magic to take down the Kings. In the end, it required the combined magic of two Druids from Moreann's realm, two Druids from Earth, and both a Dark's and Light's Fae power to finally cause havoc for the Kings.

Rordan smiled. "But even that wasn't enough."

With the death of both Moreann and Usaeil, the Others had been defeated and disbanded. Or at least they should have been. It seemed the Druids and Fae on Earth had gotten a taste of power and what merging magic could get them. Now, both the Druids and the Fae were trying to organize their own groups of Others.

Which was why Rordan was currently in Keel. The small village on Achill Island on the west side of Ireland was scenic, but he would rather be reaping souls or searching for Xaneth. Yet it wasn't his call. Death wanted someone to infiltrate this fledgling organization. Eoghan, the leader of Rordan's group of Reapers, had chosen him for the task. Most everyone else in his group was still hunting for Xaneth.

Rordan shook his head. He wasn't convinced that the royal Light Fae was still alive. They might have found where Usaeil, his aunt, had held him, but there hadn't been a body. And knowing Usaeil as they all did, no doubt she had executed her nephew. The more Rordan thought about it, the more he thought it might be better for Xaneth if he had been killed. Because if the Fae was alive, there was no telling what Usaeil had done to mess with him.

But that wasn't Rordan's mission. He drew in a deep breath and stood on the white-sand beach and stared out over the waters of the Atlantic as the moon glinted off the surface, making the light shimmer in otherworldly radiance.

The night before, he had attended the first meeting under the guise of rebuilding the Fae into a unified species. The entire night had been filled with words about uniting the Light and Dark Fae, about returning to one great race as they had been initially. Not once had it been touted that it had anything to do with the Others. But then again, that would be too obvious. The ringleader of this group was cautious and diligent in who made it to the future gatherings. From what little Rordan and the Reapers had gleaned, the first two meetings were meant to see who wanted more. After that, it was by invitation only.

Though Feardorcha, or Dorcha as everyone called him, was the frontman, Rordan wasn't sure that he was the one pulling the strings. Dorcha might have a way with words and could sway others to his way of thinking, but did he have the brains to back it up and run the Fae Others? Rordan planned to find out.

The heavy security in the first meeting had been enough to alert Rordan that much more was going on with Dorcha and his silver tongue. Though he had to hand it to the Light. He had a gift for words the likes of which Rordan had rarely seen. With one sentence, Dorcha could seemingly sway an entire room to whatever he wanted. It wasn't just what he said but also the way he spoke. Everyone knew that Dorcha felt everything he said.

Even Rordan.

He ran a hand over his jaw as he considered his next move. Gaining access to the first meeting had been easy. Every Fae in Keel had been invited. Rordan was surprised at how many Fae were in the village, living alongside the humans. On such an isle, Rordan would've thought to find only one or two Light. Instead, there were over a dozen, with more that came from the neighboring village, as well as from the surrounding isles.

Rordan thought about Dorcha's talk the previous night, of how the Fae should empower themselves. Much of what he said went hand-in-hand with what Rhi and Noreen attempted. To cease having any one person rule the Light or the Dark, and instead have a governing council made up of both sects of the Fae. Things weren't going as smoothly as everyone had hoped, though. There was too much hostility and hatred between the Light and the Dark, and it had begun eons ago. Therefore, change wasn't so readily accepted.

In fact, Rordan wasn't sure those obstacles could be overcome, but he agreed that a council was the best course of action to move the Fae forward. If Rordan weren't in Keel to spy on Dorcha and his clandestine organization, he would've said that Dorcha was someone who should be on the council. And that worried him.

Rordan's gaze lifted to the moon. It was nearly time for the second meeting. This would be when Dorcha went deeper into his thoughts. Instead of highlighting all the things that were wrong with the Fae and his very brief outlook on how they could change, Rordan suspected this would be when Dorcha began the talk that would eventually lead to information about the Others and how to join.

The problem was, Rordan wasn't sure how many sessions it would take before he got to the final meeting and was able to infiltrate the Others. Or if he could. Which meant he had to show that he believed every word Dorcha spoke that evening.

Eoghan and Death didn't expect him to infiltrate the Others, but Rordan saw an opportunity. The Reapers simply wanted to know who was running things so they could take care of them. But Rordan knew that unless he became one of the Others, the Reapers might not be able to stop them before they grew too large.

If they hadn't already.

While a Reaper's duty was to collect the souls of the Fae Death judged, the Reapers juggled many more tasks. Rordan didn't mind any of it. He was grateful to have gotten a second chance, and that chance had come because Death had seen something in him that he didn't see in himself. It was only because of her that he hadn't turned into something else entirely.

And it was one of the reasons he would never question anything Death said or did. Even though being one of her Reapers required such a vow, he would've given it regardless. Death, Eoghan, and all the Reapers were his family—the only one that mattered now.

His thoughts turned back to his mission. So much hinged on gaining access to Dorcha and those who ran this new group. The original Others had been secretive. It had taken a lot for the Dragon Kings to uncover the organization and their plot to kill the Kings. Given that the Others had kept who they were confidential, how had the Fae and Druids found out about them?

This wasn't a new situation that had come about only after the original Others had been stopped. The group Rordan currently investigated had been in place for some time now. Which meant they had known about the Others for much, much longer than anyone else.

That's what disturbed him. Death might be a goddess and have Cael—Reaper-turned-god—beside her, but she wasn't all-knowing. If she were, then this new threat would've been dealt with before it had time to gain ground.

Then there was the fact that no one really knew what the Others wanted. Couple that with the Druids starting their own group of Others, and it made it challenging for Rordan to think of anything else. Although the Druids weren't Death's problem—or at least they weren't for the time being. Things changed frequently, and the best thing he'd learned was to accept whatever change happened and learn to adjust…and quickly.

He turned and looked over his shoulder. The lights from the nearby homes and the village could be seen, and he could just make out the top of the cottage he was using on the cliff above him. He had remained at the beach for as long as he could so he would arrive late to Moorehall, just as he wanted. Hopefully, it would make everyone believe that he hadn't quite made up his mind until the last minute.

He looked at the ocean once more and released a long breath. It was nice here. He wished he could veil himself so no one could see him, but if someone was watching, they would notice. And he suspected that the Fae were being watched. He couldn't bring any attention to himself. It had been a very long time since he'd walked so casually among his own kind. Usually, he was veiled so no one saw him. He preferred it that way.

Rordan could no longer tarry. He teleported to Moorehall before he changed his mind. He appeared a hundred feet in front of the main entrance. Lights mimicking flames flickered near the doorway. He looked around but saw no humans anywhere. Rumors in the village were that the manor was haunted. It kept most mortals away. Those who ventured too close were usually repelled by Fae magic. And those humans had no idea how lucky they were. Had the Fae here been Dark, any who got close would have been lured in to become a meal since the Dark consumed human souls by having sex with the mortals.

Rordan walked to the entrance. As he neared, the door opened of its own accord. The moment he crossed the threshold, he spotted two guards on either side of the door. They were the ones who wanted to be seen. With a quick glance, Rordan spotted another four stationed in hidden areas about the foyer and on the second floor.

He made his way to the ballroom. There weren't quite as many Fae as the night before, but still more than he had expected. It just proved how good Dorcha was at attracting those who wanted something to believe in. As Rordan looked around, he spotted faces he hadn't seen the night before. That's when he realized that these were more than likely Fae who had come from other places for the second meeting.

This time, he decided to remain in the back of the room to better survey the entirety of the space and those within—even the Fae who thought they were out of sight. The conversation was kept to a minimum as everyone waited for Dorcha. Rordan declined a drink offer from a passing servant and crossed his arms over his chest.

The ceiling arched high overhead and sported a mural of Fae in various stages of undress and sexual positions. A narrow balcony ran the entirety of the ballroom's perimeter, where guards were strategically posted, watching the event—concealed, of course. Six sets of soaring windows ran along the outer wall that opened to a courtyard. Elegant, white silk curtains framed the windows and were drawn back by several strands of pearls and gold chain. Rordan counted six doors in all.

The walls had been painted a muted gold with more murals of naked Fae. Decorative finishes accented the underside of the balcony, the columns, and the doorframes. Five colossal gold chandeliers sporting hanging lightbulbs that looked like pearls were suspended from the ceiling in a mix of modern and luxurious. The floor was white marble with a gold trim border. The stage stood at the other end of the ballroom.

There were no chairs. And only three servants moved about the room, offering refreshments. To anyone looking, it seemed nothing more than a casual get-together. It was anything but.

One of the doors near the stage drew Rordan's gaze. To his surprise, he spotted the same petite female from the night before. She kept to the shadows like the rest of the guards. He wanted to let his gaze linger on her, but that wouldn't be wise. Besides, he had gotten a good look last night. Heart-shaped face made more severe by the slicked-back bun of black hair. Large eyes of the palest silver seemed to miss nothing. Her lips were unnaturally full and wide, the kind of mouth that would make anyone get on their knees and beg for a taste. She wore dark, shapeless clothes that helped her to blend in with the shadows. All in all, she exuded a no-nonsense attitude that shouldn't make her alluring.

But fek if it didn't.

Rordan inwardly shook himself. Now was not the time to focus on anything but his mission. He set about trying to see how many attendees he recognized from the night before. Out of the thirty that had come the previous evening, nearly twenty—including himself—had returned.

He spotted movement and saw the intriguing female slip from her spot at the same time Dorcha walked into the room. Rordan made himself clap, but he kept his gaze on the female as she moved around the edge of the room. To his surprise, he saw her direct other guards to new locations.

"A beauty, isn't she?"

Rordan snapped his head around to find a male beside him. Rordan raised a brow. "Excuse me?"

The other male smiled and tipped his head toward the female. "You aren't the only one watching. But if you're smart, you'll stay away before they tell you to."

Now Rordan was *really* interested. "Until who tells me to?"

"Dorcha and his men." The Fae held out his hand. "I'm Ruarc."

"Rordan. Why does Dorcha care about the female?"

Ruarc's lips curved into a smile. "That's his sister. Fianna."

"How is it you know so much about them?"

Ruarc shrugged and clasped his hands behind his back. "I helped them find Moorehall to host the meetings."

"So, you know them well?"

Ruarc thought about that for a moment and then shook his head. "I wouldn't say that. I don't think I've shared one word with Fianna. She keeps to herself, and Dorcha makes sure no one goes near her."

"She's surrounded tonight."

"Because she's his head of security."

Now that was fascinating. Rordan glanced her way to see that she had placed guards in more strategic locations than the previous night, proving that she saw the differences between the two crowds and took action.

Ruarc leaned close. "The siblings have been in the area for almost three months. In all that time, I've never seen her anywhere but at Dorcha's side. From what the other guards say, she's very good at her job."

"How many of these meetings have you attended?" Rordan asked, turning his attention away from Fianna and back to Ruarc. He wasn't certain of the male's objective, and it was better that he not give anyone something to worry about.

"This is my second, like you."

Rordan quirked a brow. "How would you know that?"

Ruarc's lips widened into a smile. "Observation. The second meetings are held on Wednesdays. If you can't make one week, then you go to the next."

"So you've known them for three months, helped them find this place, and you weren't able to attend until now? I find that difficult to believe."

"I had obligations that required my attention. My time is significantly constrained. When I do get free time, I'm exceedingly selective about how I spend it."

"I can understand that." If Ruarc were telling the truth. Rordan still wasn't sure about that.

Their conversation ceased as Dorcha finally got onto the stage after having a brief conversation with someone. Rordan tried to listen, but he found his attention diverted, moving to Fianna and wondering how long her hair would be if he took it down.

CHAPTER THREE

He was back. Fianna wasn't sure how she felt about it. She spotted the Fae speaking to Ruarc, and the first thing that popped into her head was that she could find out the male's name now. The minute that filled her thoughts, she knew she hadn't overcome her interest from the night before.

Hopefully, he wouldn't return for the third meeting. She didn't want to have to ask Dorcha to send him away. Not only would that alert her brother—and father since Dorcha told him everything—but if Dorcha thought the Fae would benefit their cause, then he would ignore her request.

Fek. She hated this. All of it. But just like the previous night, she would triumph. Because she had no other choice.

The rest of the evening went as planned. There were no disturbances, which she should be happy about, but she wasn't. The simple truth was that she needed a distraction. And nothing could keep her mind off the handsome Fae no matter how much she wished otherwise. Time and again, she found her gaze pulled to the male.

Time and again, she wished he was looking at her.

And every time, she knew she was putting herself in a position to fall into the same snare that had gotten her mother.

Her control was quickly slipping away. Fianna felt real panic. She wasn't sure she could make it to the end of the night. She might have to leave. It would cause a scene, something her brother detested above all else. It felt like an eternity before she heard Dorcha wrapping up the meeting.

Fianna released a grateful sigh and closed her eyes for a brief second. She had gained another victory, although it was one she would keep to herself—just as the one from the night before. Keeping them a secret made them much more extraordinary, in her opinion.

Her eyes snapped open to find that Dorcha wasn't leaving the room as he normally did. Instead, he had gotten off the stage to mingle with the guests. He didn't usually do this until those who were chosen were initiated into the organization. She stared at him, silently demanding that he look her way.

A few moments later, her sibling turned his head to her. He shot her a smile that made her roll her eyes. She hated when he changed things up. He said he only did it when it was called for, but she knew he did it to keep her on her toes. Ugh. Brothers. They could be such arses.

Fianna observed as Dorcha paused and spoke to those who came to him. She never got tired of watching him answer questions, then direct the individual in such a way that the person actually believed they were the ones who ended the conversation. Dorcha had that kind of sway over just about everyone except for her and their father.

Her thoughts came to a halt when she realized who Dorcha was going to see—Ruarc. Who still stood next to the hot Fae.

She inwardly cringed. Had she really just thought *hot*? Shite.

In a matter of moments, Dorcha was alone with Ruarc and the other Fae, the rest of the guests having departed. She wanted to go to them and hear the conversation, but she never did such things. Fianna swallowed and motioned to the guards on the opposite side of the room to check the house. Sentries were already around the wooded estate to make sure that no one remained.

Dorcha's charismatic personality and charming behavior had men and women alike flocking to him endlessly. On more than one occasion, she had escorted Fae from their location after they tried to reach Dorcha. It didn't matter how many times they told her that they were the one meant for her brother, she always rolled her eyes.

Unlike her, Dorcha kept on the straight and narrow, never deviating. Not once had he ever given their father cause for worry. Nor had Dorcha needed to be watched or locked in a room as she had. But that was many, many centuries ago. She had survived and overcome everything to stand where she was now. Nothing—and *no one*—would jeopardize that.

Fianna grew tired of waiting for her brother to finish speaking to Ruarc and the Fae. Other guards in the ballroom could watch him. And Dorcha knew enough to handle himself should anything happen. With that, she spun and made her way to the kitchen. She was starving, and there was no need to wait to eat any longer.

She nodded to the cook and looked over the array of finger foods, choosing several appetizers. She grabbed a glass of red wine sitting on a tray and leaned against the wall. Despite her internal struggle, things had been going really well in Keel. Usually, they stayed in an area for three to four months before they moved on to another. A part of her hoped that once Dorcha finished the last meeting on Friday, he would tell her they were moving to the next location. Although he never made those decisions. That was all their father, Fearghal. He, like she, preferred to remain in the background. Her father rarely left his house, nor did he allow any visitors other than his children.

Fianna hoped she didn't get that bad. Then again, there was nothing wrong with being a hermit. It would keep her out of trouble.

And keep trouble away from her.

She finished the wine and set the glass down as she wiped her hands on a napkin. No doubt Ruarc and the male were long gone by now. Fianna spent much of a day getting ready for meetings. It wasn't until the end of the night that she allowed herself to rest and take a few hours of alone time.

Fianna walked back to the ballroom to find it empty. It was like a huge weight had been lifted from her shoulders. She pivoted and made her way to the entryway and up the stairs to her room. There, she slipped off her boots and was about to take off her shirt when she looked out her window and spotted the moon. She had wanted to swim in Lough Carra since they arrived. Tonight was as good a time as any.

Fianna teleported to the lake. With a simple thought, her clothes vanished. She was about to call a bathing suit to her when she stopped. There was nothing wrong with swimming naked.

Da wouldn't like it. You know that. He'd tell you not to tread so close to the line.

Fianna couldn't ignore the logic of her subconscious. She used her magic to call a white, one-piece bathing suit to cover herself. Then she walked into the cool lough. She smiled and moved deeper until the water reached her chest. Then she dove. Fianna swam until her lungs burned. Only then did she break the surface and suck in a mouthful of air.

For the next hour, she leisurely swam and floated beneath the moonlight. It did wonders to soothe her and right her both emotionally and mentally. She could've remained all night, but she knew she had to get back. Fianna walked from the water, and with a snap of her fingers, the bathing suit was gone, and her clothes were back in place.

Instead of teleporting to her room, she decided to walk because she wasn't quite ready to give up the beauty and solitude of the night. She found it humorous that so many humans feared the darkness. Then again, if she didn't have magic, she might be afraid of it, as well.

She was nearing the manor when she heard voices. Fianna halted, listening. It was then that she heard her brother. Curious, she walked toward the sound and found him speaking to one of her guards. Lewis had been with them only a few months, and like many, was utterly devoted to Dorcha.

Fianna frowned when her brother put his arm around the guard and drew him close. At that exact moment, Lewis looked up and spotted her. He jerked back, which caused Dorcha to turn his head to her.

"Are you spying on me?" her brother demanded.

She raised a brow. "I was out for a walk and heard voices. I was doing my job and investigating it."

"I don't need you to watch over me every second."

It took everything she had not to roll her eyes. "Oddly enough, I once said the same thing. Do you remember your reply?"

Dorcha's always-smiling lips flattened in fury. "I do," he said between clenched teeth.

"Then I don't need to remind you." Fianna looked at Lewis before returning her gaze to Dorcha.

Her brother cut the guard a glance and whispered something she didn't hear. Without another look her way, Lewis turned on his heel and left.

Fianna walked to Dorcha and glared up at him. "If you have an issue with one of my guards, you should tell me instead of going to them yourself."

Dorcha blinked, staring at her as if he didn't understand. Then, in an instant, his fury was gone. "You're right. I shouldn't have done that."

"What did Lewis do?"

"I just wanted to caution him about trusting our guests too easily."

Fianna was confused. "I chose every one of the guards. I

questioned them endlessly and trained them myself. They all know not to trust anyone until they become one of us."

"You're right. I apologize for stepping into your domain," Dorcha said with a bow of his head. He then looked at her with a smile. "Forgive me?"

She could never stay angry at him for long. "Of course."

He held out his arms, and she walked to him, wrapping her arm around his waist as they strolled back to the house. They hadn't always gotten along. She was happy that they could do so now. She wasn't sure what she would do without him. He, like their father, was the most important thing in her life.

"Your hair is wet," Dorcha said.

She nodded and glanced up at him. "I went for a swim."

"You're supposed to tell me where you're going."

"I needed some alone time."

"I did as well. But tell me next time. How was the water?"

She sighed wistfully. "Wonderful. You should try it."

"I will soon."

Once in the house, Dorcha grabbed her hand to stop her when she went to walk away. She became worried when she saw the frown on his face. "What is it?"

"You do a great job for me. For our group. I'm not sure I tell you that enough."

She shrugged but was pleased. "Thank you."

"You're a vital part of all of this. You know that, don't you?"

Fianna laughed, but Dorcha's frown remained in place. "I'm not the one who calls others to join us. I'm not the one who knows just what to say to the right people to grow our ranks. That's you."

Dorcha made an indiscriminate sound.

"You need to rest," she told him.

He nodded and released her to make his way to his room. She waited until he was out of sight before she took a deep breath and smiled. Dorcha's compliment was the first she had gotten in decades. It felt good.

So very good.

CHAPTER FOUR

The person Rordan couldn't take his mind off of wasn't Dorcha, but rather his sister, Fianna. Rordan walked the long stretch of beach in the morning sun, letting the waves roll over his bare feet. He should be contemplating the fact that Dorcha had approached him the previous evening, yet his mind remained on Fianna.

The female drew his attention like none before her. He wasn't sure if it was because she ignored him or if it was something more. The few times her gaze had landed on him made him feel as if he had been scorched—and he didn't think that was a particularly bad thing.

Fianna didn't just intrigue him. She fascinated him, captivated him. *Enthralled* him to the point that he couldn't focus on anything else. And he knew he had to find out more about her, talk to her. The more he kept his distance, the more this…interest…would grow until it engulfed him.

"Fek me," Rordan murmured as he halted and turned to face the water.

He glanced to the side and saw a mortal couple with a dog. They laughed as the animal rushed into the waves after a ball, then bounded back to them with tail wagging. It triggered a memory from his childhood and his dog. He frowned, wondering why the memory had suddenly come to him. He hadn't thought about his past—specifically his childhood—in, well…ages. Some things were better left undisturbed.

Rordan turned his head to the other side, hoping that no longer seeing the dog would make the memories go away. He spotted another figure, this one approaching him. He recognized Ruarc. The Fae smiled as he drew closer but stopped short of standing next to Rordan so his shoes wouldn't get wet.

"Why do I get the feeling you were looking for me?" Rordan asked.

Ruarc chuckled and stuck his hands into his pants' pockets. "Because I was."

"Why?"

"You know why. Dorcha wants an answer."

Rordan ran his hand over the top of his hair. "I didn't take him for the pushy type."

"He usually isn't."

Now that certainly got Rordan's attention. "Why now?"

Ruarc twisted his lips and said in a voice filled with concern, "I don't know."

Rordan turned to face the Fae. "What do you think about all of it?"

"You don't appear the type to trust easily, and we barely know each other. That means you're asking my opinion to see if I'll say something that will either agree with your assessment or not."

Rordan didn't hide his smile. He liked Ruarc.

Ruarc grinned and shook his head. "I'd do the same in your shoes. Like I told you last night, I don't know Dorcha or Fianna well. You saw for yourself that his sister keeps away from others. It hasn't been easy getting a read on them."

"That isn't typically something you hear just any Fae say."

Ruarc's silver gaze slid away to look at the ocean. "Sometimes our paths lead us to things we want. Other times, the things we think we want lead us down paths we wish we never would've traveled upon."

"You seem to have done all right."

"Looks can be deceiving." Ruarc returned his gaze to Rordan. "Suffice it to say that I wasn't always just a Fae who procured places for other Fae to live."

Rordan nodded slowly. "I think you're much more than that even now."

Ruarc looked at the couple with the dog. "The one thing about humans is that their life spans are so short. They don't usually realize they've fekked it all up until it's too late. Hopefully, they'll learn their lesson in the next life, but it's a toss-up. For the Fae, we live such long lives that we know where it's all been buggered and we can fix it."

"The operative word there is *can*," Rordan interjected.

Ruarc chuckled and glanced his way. "Exactly. You have no reason to trust me, but you asked me a question so I'll answer. Last night was only my second meeting. I think Dorcha was a bit put off that I hadn't returned sooner. He truly believes in the message he's sending."

Rordan wanted to ask Ruarc if he thought the message was about bringing the Fae together as Dorcha made it sound from the last two gatherings, but he thought better of it, at least for the time being. Ruarc was opening up, and only time would tell if Rordan could trust him.

"From the look of surprise I saw on Fianna's face," Ruarc continued, "I don't think Dorcha usually goes out to greet the guests. But that's just my take on it."

"And what Dorcha said to you?" Rordan asked.

"You mean to *us*?" Ruarc corrected, a black brow raised. "I don't know. The house is obviously vast enough to accommodate a large number of people. And I can't say for certain that he hasn't invited anyone to stay with him before, but it does seem…odd."

Rordan crossed his arms over his chest. "Like maybe he wants to keep an eye on us?"

"Or he's that interested in us joining his organization."

Rordan grunted. "I suppose that could go either way. What are you going to do?"

"I have a house here."

"That doesn't answer my question."

Ruarc's lips split in a smile as he laughed. "I have a feeling if I don't agree, things might not go so well for me. Dorcha brings in good business, and I've got several other locations he's going to visit. It would be in my best interest to accept his offer. What about you?"

Rordan thought about Fianna then quickly shoved her aside. His mission was to get inside this new organization. He couldn't do that by keeping his distance, no matter how much the thought of joining them made him sick to his stomach. Dorcha's offer made his mission easier, and that didn't happen often. He'd be a fool to let this pass.

"I'm going to accept."

Ruarc's eyes widened in surprise. "I wasn't expecting that."

"Me, either."

Ruarc's surprise shifted to wariness. "Then why do it?"

"Because Dorcha intrigues me. Why else would I go to a second meeting?"

"I suppose." Ruarc drew in a deep breath, his shoulders lifting. "I'm headed there in a few hours." Ruarc started to turn away then paused and met Rordan's gaze once more. "Watch yourself."

Rordan bowed his head. "I always do."

The Light Fae nodded, then retraced his steps to disappear over the doon. Rordan's gaze remained on the spot for a long time, thinking over his exchange with Ruarc. The more he talked to the Fae, the more he liked him. Rordan hadn't felt such a kinship with anyone but the Reapers since he had joined their ranks. He was surprised by his reaction to Ruarc.

Then again, there was also Rordan's attraction to Fianna. He would have to deal with that immediately because the last thing he needed was such a distraction.

Rordan remained on the beach for a little longer. When more humans arrived, he took his leave, returning to the small wind-swept cottage nearby. He quite liked the quaint home situated atop the cliff. He had yet to pick a place on Death's realm for himself, but when he did, he wanted a cottage much like this one. It was simple, which was all he needed.

Once he made sure that everything was as it had been when he moved in, Rordan teleported to Moorehall once more. When he arrived, he looked at the entrance and the stone steps leading to the front door. As if on cue, the panels opened, and Dorcha filled the entrance.

"Ruarc said you were coming," Dorcha said with a smile.

Rordan knew he was walking into a viper's nest. His abilities as a Reaper would keep him alive longer than a regular Fae, but that didn't mean Fae magic couldn't kill him. And he knew better than to believe that he wouldn't eventually be attacked. His secrets would only remain with him for so long. He stood a better chance of keeping them to himself if he kept his distance from Dorcha and the Others, but if he were to complete his mission, he had to leap in headfirst.

"I'm still confused as to why you invited me," Rordan said once he had climbed the steps and stood before Dorcha.

The Fae smiled and patted him on the back. "I'm very good a reading people, and I see something special in you."

Rordan wished he believed that he had deceived Dorcha well enough that the Light had no clue that he was a spy. But Rordan tried his best never to underestimate anyone. At least, not anymore. He had trusted everyone at one point in his life. The end result of that had changed him drastically.

"You doubt me?" Dorcha said when Rordan didn't reply.

Rordan shrugged. "I like what you said at the last two meetings. It's why I'm here."

"And I want you to have the ability to learn more before the third one. Come in, come in. Let me show you to your room."

Rordan followed Dorcha inside the house. It looked the same as the previous two times he had been inside, but this time, his eyes scanned the area for a glimpse of Fianna. He knew she was around somewhere, and Rordan could imagine that, as head of security, she wasn't happy to have guests in the house.

"You and Ruarc aren't the only guests," Dorcha told him as he led the way up the curving staircase to the second floor of the manor. "There are five more who will join us."

"Do you usually invite others into your home?"

Dorcha chuckled and glanced over his shoulder at Rordan. "This is our home only as long as we're here. But to answer your question, nay. This is a first because I wanted to try something different. You see, what I'm endeavoring to do is vital to our survival." He stopped when he reached the landing and waited for Rordan to fall into step with him. Then he continued walking and said, "What I foresee for our people can happen now with the right individuals moving such an initiative forward."

Curious to see his reaction, Rordan asked, "Is that not already taking place? There are Fae already attempting to get a council of Dark and Light together to rule all instead of a king or queen."

"I think it's a step in the right direction," Dorcha answered succinctly. "But I believe there are flaws in how it's being done. That's why there's so much resistance."

"You have a better idea?"

The Light flashed him a wide smile as he stopped beside a door. "I do. And I'm going to share that with you. This will be your room while you remain with us. Please, make yourself at home. Go anywhere you'd like on the estate."

"What of the security I saw?"

"The guards are here for my protection."

Rordan quirked a brow. "Are you saying there are those who want you dead?"

"Let's just say that not everyone agrees with what I'm trying to do. You have nothing to fear, however. Fianna, my sister, is an expert at security."

"And if I do agree to join you? Does that mean I'll also have to worry about someone attacking me?"

Dorcha smiled and shook his head. "By the time I have everyone amassed as needed, we'll have nothing to fear. I'll leave you to it."

Rordan watched as Dorcha walked away and started down the stairs before he entered the room and looked around. It was spacious with a truly revolting floral comforter and curtains that he would have a difficult time ignoring. He walked to the window and looked out to the back of the manor. Rordan spotted the shimmer of water in the distance. Lough Carra. The six-mile-long freshwater lake drew humans and Fae alike. He would have to take a walk there later and get a better look at it.

For now, he wanted to look around the manor. If he were lucky, he'd run into Ruarc.

Or Fianna.

CHAPTER FIVE

With her hands braced on either side of the sink, Fianna took in huge mouthfuls of air as she tried to calm herself. This couldn't be happening.

Oh, but it is.

She squeezed her eyes closed. Fianna attempted to discern what her brother had been thinking, inviting others to the manor. But no matter how hard she tried, she couldn't. Worse, he had invited the handsome Fae.

Rordan.

The name rolled through her mind like a seductive whisper. She slammed her hand on the sink to make it stop. But the damage had already been done. She opened her eyes and straightened to look at herself in the mirror.

"You can do this," she told herself. "You're stronger. Look what you overcame. You know better than to give in to the demons like before. Besides, Dorcha relies on you. So does Da. You won't let either of them down."

You sure about that?

"I can do this. I'm stronger than before. I won't give in to the demons. And I won't let Da or Dorcha down," she repeated the mantra, this time with conviction.

Thankfully, her subconscious remained quiet for the moment. No doubt it would return at an inopportune occasion, but she was prepared for that. What she wasn't prepared for was having to speak to Rordan or any of the others. Dorcha knew her preferences. Surely, he wouldn't force her to have dinner with everyone.

"Surely."

But she wasn't so certain. Fianna squared her shoulders, walked from the restroom, and tidied her already perfectly organized room before walking out. Her first stop was the perimeter of the manor. With guests now at the house, Dorcha had forced her to move the guards away so their guests could move about freely without seeing the security at every turn. Frankly, she thought it was better if everyone knew the guards were there. But Dorcha had overruled her. As he always did.

She made her way to each of the guards, checking between their stations as she went. Everything was in order, but she inspected everything twice just to be sure—and as a reason to stay away from the manor. When she headed back, she found herself trying to think of anything that might keep her busy and out of the house. She heard the sounds of sparring. A smile pulled at her lips as she hurried to the training area she had set up for herself and the guards to use for hand-to-hand and magical sparring.

Fianna stretched as she watched Leo and Ella face each other for some hand-to-hand training. It was Fianna's favorite kind. Magic came easily to the Fae—too easy, in her opinion. Going at a foe and forcing close-range combat, usually put them off balance and allowed her a victory.

Ella was quick, and she used that to her advantage, but she was also predictable, and Leo ended up winning the scuffle.

"I know, I know," Ella said with a twist of her lips when she spotted Fianna. She got to her feet and dusted herself off. "I'm predictable."

Leo wore a cocky smile. "Very."

Fianna laughed. "Good job, Leo, but be mindful that Ella could be leading you to believe she's predictable—until she's not."

The two guards bowed to her and moved away. Fianna walked to the center of the arena and waited to see who would join her. To her delight, two male guards came at her.

To say that Rordan was impressed with Fianna was an understatement. He and the rest of the Reapers were some of the best warriors among the Fae, but Fianna was good enough to hold her own with them. Her movements were fluid, her attacks decisive and quick. The two males attacked her in different ways, and Fianna not only stayed on her feet but also easily shifted from one attack to the other.

"How did I know I'd find you here?"

Rordan looked over to find Ruarc staring at him, a smile in place. Rordan chuckled and made sure to remain hidden behind the tree so Fianna couldn't see him. "You must have heard them as I did."

"I knew it was training, and I had a feeling Fianna would be here. Which meant, I suspected you'd be here."

Rordan's attention returned to Fianna. He wanted to get in there and train with her, to see how far he could push her—and what moves she kept to herself. "I was having a look around the grounds. The estate is impressive."

"It is. A beautiful forest surrounds the manor, and then there's Lough Carra."

"I caught a glimpse of it from my window."

"I'm sure if you want to join in, Fianna wouldn't mind."

There was a smile in Ruarc's voice that made Rordan look at him. "Why do you say that?"

"Because I've been around warriors, and you clearly wish to spar."

He did. "I'm fine."

Ruarc's smile died as he swung his gaze to Fianna and the other guards. He shifted to make sure he was hidden, as well.

Rordan studied him for a moment. "What's on your mind?"

"Nothing," Ruarc replied and glanced in his direction.

Rordan quirked a brow. "You were right earlier. We don't know each other well, but I suspect you're very good at your current occupation. That leads me to believe you don't necessarily need the money from Dorcha."

"Looks can be deceiving."

"I know that better than most," Rordan retorted.

Ruarc met his gaze and lowered his voice. "Dorcha is gaining popularity."

"Apparently, he's not that popular if he needs security."

"He's influential and has the backing of the kind of Fae others rarely mess with."

Rordan frowned. This was new information. "What kind of Fae?"

"The dangerous kind."

"Are you worried they'll retaliate against you if you decline Dorcha's offer?"

Ruarc shrugged and moved closer. "I've made plenty of mistakes, but the one thing I've always done is trust my instincts."

"What are they telling you now?"

"The same thing yours did this morning—run."

Rordan turned to face Ruarc and leaned a shoulder against the tree. "Then you should heed your instincts."

"You aren't."

Rordan really didn't want to lie to Ruarc, but at this point, he didn't have a choice. "I'm interested in Dorcha's philosophies. I

think a unified Fae is what's best for us. For too long, it has been
Light against Dark. Imagine all the enemies of the Fae who have
been able to strike at the heart of us simply because we've been in a
near-constant state of civil war. Now envision a world where we
stand together and face those enemies as one."

"I agree. I think the Fae need to be united."

Not under Dorcha was left unsaid. Rordan nodded as he studied
Ruarc. He suspected that the Fae had more he wanted to say, but
since he didn't trust Rordan, Ruarc kept it to himself. Rordan
wished he could convince Ruarc that he could be trusted but
assuring someone of something didn't make it so. Trust had to be
earned.

"You've taken a risk telling me all of this," Rordan said,
suddenly wary.

Ruarc blew out a breath and looked back at the sparring ring. "I
haven't said anything I wouldn't repeat to Dorcha or anyone else."

That wasn't entirely true, but Rordan didn't press the issue. "If
you were wondering, I won't repeat what you've told me to anyone."

"Things appear to be everything Dorcha says they are." Ruarc's
head swung to Rordan, and their gazes met.

There, in the Fae's dark silver eyes, Rordan saw that he wasn't
sure everything *was* as it appeared to be. Rordan realized that Ruarc
trusted him with this. If Rordan kept it to himself, then he had
gained some ground with the Fae. If Rordan went to anyone with it,
all Ruarc had to say was that Rordan had read too much into the
statement.

"Is there a meeting tonight?" Rordan asked.

"Not that I'm aware. Dorcha did tell me there was to be a
dinner. I think he might use that to go into more depth with what he
has planned for the Fae."

"He told me there were four other guests, as well."

"Ah. I didn't know that." Ruarc's brows rose briefly. "It should
be an interesting evening. You sure you don't want to spar?" he
asked with a smile.

Rordan looked at Fianna to see that she had won her match and
had moved on to another. Not a single onyx strand was out of place

from her slicked-back bun, but there was a smile on her face. She enjoyed training, and not just magical sparring. Most Fae would look down on hand-to-hand, saying it was too human. Many believed that magic was the only way to battle another. Rordan had learned the hard way that when you used any and all tactics when in a scuffle. It's why he had become proficient in more than just battle magic.

"You might want to hide your blatant interest when you're around Dorcha and the others," Ruarc advised.

Rordan jerked back, realizing his mistake. He turned his back on Fianna and bowed his head to Ruarc. "Thank you for the reminder. It's been a long time since anyone caught my interest as she has."

"There's nothing wrong with that."

"I could argue the point."

Ruarc shrugged one shoulder. "Who knows? She might be attracted to you, as well."

Rordan prayed she wasn't. He heard clapping behind him and wanted to turn around and see what Fianna had done, but he made himself stay faced forward.

"Come," Ruarc suggested. "There's much more of the estate to see."

Rordan gladly followed him. The farther away from Fianna he got, the better he felt. "When did you acquire this property?"

"About three hundred years ago."

"I'm surprised you didn't choose it as your home."

Ruarc chuckled as they made their way out of the forest to the garden area. "A big house like this is great if there are others to fill it. It isn't so nice living alone."

"You don't have a mate?"

"I didn't say that," Ruarc replied. Then, in the next breath, he said, "Oddly enough, the Fae are drawn to Moorehall. It's rarely unoccupied for an extended period. Dorcha and Fianna's stay might be the shortest time anyone has leased the manor. Usually, it's occupied for at least a decade or so."

Rordan glanced at Ruarc, thinking about his comment

regarding his mate, but he didn't press the issue. It was obviously a sore subject. And Rordan knew all about keeping those kinds of things hidden away. He had plenty of those secrets himself.

Just as they left the forest, he glanced back, hoping to get one final look at Fianna, but there was nothing but trees.

"There's always tonight," Ruarc reminded him.

Suddenly, Rordan was looking forward to dinner.

CHAPTER SIX

"No."

Dorcha raised a brow. "Yes."

Fianna glared at him as they stood in her bedroom, careful to keep their voices low so their guests didn't hear. "I'm not going down to that ill-advised dinner. You want to have guests, then have them. I don't need to be there."

"You're my security."

She rolled her eyes. "All you need is a third of my guards for tonight. You don't need me."

"You're my sister. You need to be by my side."

"Since when?" she demanded. "You know I prefer not to be in

the spotlight, and now you want to thrust me into it? No. I won't do it."

Dorcha simply stared at her silently.

She hated when he was calm, and she got so riled. "I'm not going. That's final."

"You are."

"If you want me there, I'll be in the shadows like always."

"You'll be at the table with me."

Fianna took a step back. "What has gotten into you? You can't change things up like this. First, going to talk to the crowd last night. Then inviting guests to stay here. And now a dinner."

"This came from Da."

And with four words, her arguments died on her tongue. She knew better than to go against anything her father wanted—no matter how much she disagreed with it.

"That's what I thought." Dorcha blew out a breath, a satisfied look on his face.

A flash of something in his eyes made her almost question if their da really had commanded it. It wasn't as if their father spoke to her. And her brother had never lied before, so why would she think he did now? Still, she couldn't shake whatever it was that made her uncomfortable.

"You're going to dress attractively. Something elegant. None of…this," Dorcha said as he waved his hands at her usual black, boxy clothes. "You're representing our family and all we embody. People will be looking to me, to what I'm building. You'll wear white."

"I can choose my own clothes." She didn't say anything about his use of *I* when talking about the future since she was annoyed about being told what to wear.

"I disagree."

Rage filled Fianna, but she held it in. Barely. "If I'm being forced to go to this dinner, I'll wear whatever the fek I want."

Dorcha smiled at her anger. "I'll warn you now that if I don't like what you come downstairs in, I'll change your outfit myself."

With that, he turned and walked out of her room, closing the door softly behind him. She wanted to scream, to lash out and punch something. She fisted her hands instead, silently seething. There wasn't even time for her to get her temper in hand since the dinner started in a few minutes.

Fianna stripped out of her clothes and slowly laid them over the bench at the foot of her bed in an effort to get her chaotic emotions under control. Then she stood in front of the mirror and looked at herself, thinking of her brother's words.

"You want attractive and elegant, huh?" she asked the mirror. "I'll give you that and more. Then maybe you and Da won't do this to me again."

She reached behind her and released her hair. She shook it out. It had been an eternity since she'd worn it down and free and not up in some way. She didn't think she looked right with her hair loose. Her fingers itched to pull it back somehow, but she made herself leave it as it was.

Fianna bit her lip as she debated what to wear. She thought about going with black, but she knew that Dorcha would change it just because he could be an arse like that. So, she'd give him what he wanted. She smiled as she used her magic to call up the outfit and shoes. She opted for no jewelry of any kind and simply pressed her lips together to give them some color. Then she walked out of her room.

The entire walk to the dining room, her heart thumped wildly. It had been thousands of years since she had worn something like this. It felt foreign, but also…right. She couldn't help but think that it was like her old self, the one she had fought so hard to destroy, was trying to emerge. The two were polar opposites and could never be one. Besides, she had given up that old life willingly. She didn't want anything to do with it.

But dressing up and wearing heels was as exhilarating as defeating an opponent. So much so that she worried it would set her back after everything she had done to forget the person she once was—a Fae on a path to destruction and ruin.

She stopped before entering the dining room. There were voices inside. Most were male. Her thoughts skidded to Rordan and whether he was inside. She couldn't help wondering if he would like what she wore. But the minute that thought went through her mind, she inwardly shook herself. It shouldn't matter what he thought because he didn't matter.

Her subconscious gave a very loud snort in reply.

Fianna saw something out of the corner of her eye. When she looked, her gaze met Ruarc's. He had stopped mid-step, his eyes wide. A heartbeat later, he blinked and cleared his throat before giving her a nod. She bowed her head in response. He cleared his throat a second time as he walked into the room.

She couldn't be sure if he liked what he saw or if she had done too much. Maybe she should've let Dorcha choose her clothes. She wrinkled her nose at the thought. She could dress herself. If her brother didn't like what she wore and changed it, she would change it back. And if he did it again, she'd leave. Her role wasn't to play hostess to others. That was Dorcha's duty.

After a deep breath that she slowly released, she walked into the dining room. No one noticed her at first. With only six others in the room, they had broken off into pairs, most holding some sort of alcoholic beverage. Fianna glanced around for her brother and found Ruarc staring at her once more. And he wasn't alone. Beside him was none other than Rordan, wearing a black suit with a pale gray dress shirt open at the collar.

Fianna tried to look away from his silver eyes, but she couldn't do it. The appreciation she saw in his gaze helped her shake off the last of her apprehension. It had been a long, long time since a male had looked at her like that. She had nearly forgotten what it felt like.

Careful.

She was being cautious. She wasn't talking to him, merely looking and liking that he seemed to enjoy what she had chosen to wear.

A hand landed on her back, causing her to jerk her head to the side to see who dared touch her. She spotted Dorcha and met his gaze, noting his tight smile.

"I have to admit," he whispered, "I'm pleasantly surprised. I thought I'd have to carry through with my threat."

She often got irritated with her brother, but it had been a significant stretch of time since she had been this furious with him. The anger burned within her to the point that she wanted to walk away from him.

"Smile," he ordered. "People are staring."

Her lips curved into a grin, but her voice was laced with ire as she whispered, "I don't care."

"That's a lie. You're as invested in the future as I am."

She followed him with her eyes as he moved away, incensed that his words were true, and that he could get her to do whatever he wanted. Fianna swallowed and squared her shoulders. Her gaze moved to her guards, stationed around the room. More were peppered throughout the manor, with others around the property. Dorcha thought she went to extremes with the Fae she hired to protect him, but she wanted to be prepared for anything. The scenarios her father had painted for her had been horrible, and she wasn't about to lose her brother that way.

A few dangerous Fae had already taken notice of Dorcha. Those few could cause some problems and potentially make an attempt on his life as they had once done with their father. She wouldn't let that happen.

Fianna grabbed a glass of wine from a passing servant. She had fought hard to keep Dorcha's entourage to a minimum for safety's sake. However, he and their father had disagreed with her. Their egos needed the servants around to give the appearance that their family was still great and mighty—when, in fact, it wasn't.

No matter how she argued the point, the two refused to listen. It made her job that much harder because she also had to keep an eye on the servants. They were as likely as anyone to be blackmailed into either an attempt on Dorcha's life or to report back to someone. It was such a concern that she had the servants followed whenever they left the manor. Her guards had a difficult time, especially when they teleported away or used a Fae doorway.

Thankfully, nothing had come of it. She liked to plan for the worst and hope for the best. Their family had been through so much turmoil—some of it her fault. She wouldn't be the cause of any more upheaval or disgrace to them.

Fianna was used to being hidden as she watched others. Now, she was out in the open for all eyes to see. And she felt one person's in particular. Her skin heated wherever his eyes moved over her body. It became more and more challenging to keep her gaze from him. She moved to the edge of the room near the window to put some distance between her and Rordan and get herself out of the spotlight she felt was focused on her. But it didn't do any good.

Just as she was about to walk to a different location, two of Dorcha's guests stopped her—the Crowes. The couple was not only wealthy but also deeply connected to all the right Fae.

"This place is spectacular," Ayda, the wife, said.

Fianna forced a smile and took in Ayda's beaded peach column dress, noting the elaborate diamond necklace and matching earrings she wore. "That it is."

"Ruben is so in love with it, we may have to rent it for a bit once you and Dorcha are finished with it."

Fianna hated small talk of any kind. She felt it was a waste of time, but it wasn't as if she had a choice. She took in the impeccable black suit, starched white dress shirt, and diamond cufflinks Ruben wore. His hair was combed in a pompadour style that showed off his too beautiful face. "I'm sure you can set it up with Ruarc."

"We made an offer to buy it, and it was a tidy sum," Ruben said, then looked at Ayda as they shared a laugh.

Ruben wrapped his arm around his wife. "Everyone has a price. I just need to find his. Once I do, this place will be ours."

"I—" Fianna began, but the couple spoke over her.

"I keep imagining the parties we could host here," the wife said with an exaggerated sigh. "Everyone would come just to see this place."

Fianna was about to tell them that many Fae had already seen it as it had been bought and sold and rented many thousands of times over the eons, but she didn't think her brother would appreciate the snippy remark.

In an effort to curb the sarcastic retorts ready to pass her lips, she tried to excuse herself, but Ayda wouldn't let her go. The female went on and on about the different parties she'd have, how everyone would beg to visit. And her husband wasn't any better. The two were so wrapped up in themselves, they had no idea that she wasn't listening. Then again, they weren't giving her any time to respond, either.

"Excuse me."

The deep voice went through Fianna in a flash, causing a shiver of delight to rush through her like liquid heat. She turned her head to Rordan. The minute she looked into his silver eyes, she was trapped, ensnared. He stood close enough that she could feel his body heat, and she found herself wanting to lean in to him.

Fianna caught herself at the last minute. It was enough to shake her free of Rordan. At least, for the moment.

"I beg your pardon for the intrusion," Rordan told the couple. "Fianna is needed."

Ruben bowed his head. "Of course, of course."

Rordan looked at her, waiting for her to do something. Fianna turned toward him, and the two of them walked away together. She knew then that she had moved from one tricky situation into a much greater one. The only difference was, she didn't want to make Rordan shut up. It was the first time she had heard his voice, and she wanted more of it.

"You looked like a trapped animal," Rordan told her before lifting a glass of whisky to his lips.

Fianna's gaze dropped to his neck as he swallowed, watching his Adam's apple bob. "I prefer the shadows."

"Sometimes we must do things we'd rather not."

"Isn't that the truth?" she said before finishing off the last of her wine.

Rordan got her another glass and took the empty away, handing it to a servant. "I walked the grounds today and happened upon the training area. I saw you sparring with the others. You're very good."

Few ever complimented her, which made hearing it from Rordan's lips even sweeter. "Do you spar?"

"Aye."

"You should join us sometime." The second the words were out, she knew they had been a mistake, but she couldn't take them back.

To make matters worse, his lips curled in a sexy, heart-stopping smile that made the rest of the room and its occupants fall away.

"I might take you up on that offer. I'm Rordan, by the way."

She didn't hesitate to take his offered hand. His long fingers wrapped gently but firmly around hers. "Fianna."

To her surprise, she was a bit breathless, her stomach fluttering in excitement. She was treading dangerously close to a path she swore never to go down again. She pulled her hand from his and glanced around the room. Fianna noted that Dorcha was staring at her. If she didn't want to be scrutinized by her brother—or magic forbid, her father—she needed to get away from the handsome Fae.

"Thank you for helping me out," she told him, hating that she had to leave his side. "I must make the rounds."

Rordan bowed his head in reply.

Even as Fianna walked away, she knew when she crawled into bed later, she would replay the entire scene with Rordan over and over again.

CHAPTER SEVEN

By the stars, she was gorgeous. Rordan had been enraptured by her before. Now, seeing her tonight, he was beguiled. He covertly watched Fianna, noting the gentle sway of her hips as she walked, the way her lustrous, inky locks fell thick and straight to just below her shoulder blades and moved like a seductive curtain whenever she turned her head.

The simple one-shoulder, white jumpsuit fit her stunning figure, accentuating her curves without being overtly sexual. The legs of the outfit were slim and showed off her white shoes with their silver stiletto heels. The occupants of the room were predominately male, but the few women in attendance were decked out in jewels or fine metals. Not so Fianna. There wasn't a single adornment on her.

His observation was interrupted by the sound of a utensil tapping against glass. The room quieted as everyone turned to Dorcha. Only when all eyes were on him did he speak.

"This is the first time I've invited individuals to not only have a meal with me but also stay. Each of you was invited because I've seen something in you that you could potentially bring to the organization. You all know where I stand when it comes to the future of the Fae."

There were a few laughs at his statement. Rordan glanced at Fianna to find her staring at her brother as if she weren't sure what he was going to say next.

Dorcha smiled and looked at each of them. "Tonight is for celebrating new acquaintances, who will hopefully become friends. An incredible feast has been prepared that I know we're all going to enjoy. Please, find your name on the place cards and take a seat."

Ruarc came up beside Rordan. "I just know I'm going to be stuck near the Crowes. Those two don't know when to shut up."

Rordan chuckled. "Better you than me. I would tell them to zip it."

"I just might."

They walked slowly toward the long table that had been set with fine china and all the extras. Rordan had been raised in a household where they had to dress for dinner every evening. He loathed every aspect of it. More so now than ever before.

By the time he and Ruarc reached the table, there were only a few spots left. Rordan barely bit back his laugh when Ruarc was indeed situated next to the couple. But the smile vanished when Rordan found himself seated near Dorcha and across from Fianna. He had just taken his seat when the servants arrived—one to each guest—and served them simultaneously. Rordan fought not to roll his eyes.

Conversation picked up as others began on the first course. Rordan nodded to those next to him, as well as across the way. It wasn't until the second course that Dorcha turned from the two males on either side of him and made eye contact with someone down the table.

"Ruarc, I told Patrick and Casey that you would help them relocate from Dublin," Dorcha said.

Everyone glanced at Ruarc, who swallowed and wiped his mouth with his napkin. "I'll be happy to aid them as best I can. I cannot, however, promise anything. There is a lot of…disruption since both King Balladyn and Queen Usaeil were killed."

Out of his periphery, Rordan saw something dangerous flash in Dorcha's eyes. "We both know you'll come through. No matter what," Dorcha said.

Maybe it was because Rordan knew Dorcha wasn't on the up and up, but he heard the threat in the last statement, and he was sure Ruarc did, as well.

Rordan looked up to find Fianna's gaze on him. She quickly looked away, though, and turned to answer the guest next to her. He would've continued staring at her, but Dorcha chose that moment to look his way. Rordan then turned to the male on his other side and commented on how good the food was.

The other male replied in agreement, but Rordan didn't listen. His attention was on Dorcha and how he noted if anyone stared at his sister for too long. Rordan understood a brother being protective, but this seemed excessive, especially when Fianna was more than capable of handling herself.

"What brought you to Achill Island, Rordan?" Dorcha asked.

Rordan had known he would be singled out eventually, so it didn't surprise him. He waited until the servants had taken away the second course before he answered. "I came here many years ago. Someone mentioned the island, and I recalled how pretty it was. I decided to take a holiday."

"Then you heard about Dorcha," Ruben said.

Rordan glanced down the table and smiled. "Pretty much, aye."

"You don't live on the island," Dorcha replied, his elbows on the table as he steepled his hands.

There was something in his tone. Rordan met Dorcha's gaze easily. "I never said I did."

"We have people coming from all over," Fianna said. "Look at Kyle, who came all the way from Dundalk on the eastern side of Ireland."

Kyle nodded his head vigorously. "I missed Dorcha's talk when he was in town because I was away. So many of my friends were talking about him, so I found out where he was and made a point of coming."

Rordan noted the looks exchanged between the siblings. Dorcha then put a smile on his face as he sat back and lowered his hands to his lap. Talk turned to more pleasant things as the next course was brought out, but Rordan knew then that Dorcha was prying into his life. Rordan wasn't particularly worried because he could answer anything the Fae threw at him. He would have to be more vigilant, however.

He wasn't so sure Dorcha hadn't invited him to see if he could find some dirt on Rordan. He wasn't connected like the other Fae at the table—at least not in the ways Dorcha wanted. That meant that Dorcha wanted him there for other reasons—none of which could be good. If that was the case, Rordan's stay might not be as long as he'd hoped. He'd been suspicious from the instant Dorcha invited him to stay at the manor. Now, warning bells were going off in his head.

When dinner was finally finished, they all moved into another room, where everyone broke off into groups once more. He made his way to Ruarc, who had two glasses of whisky, and handed one to Rordan.

"That was painful," Ruarc whispered before he took a drink.

Rordan shrugged. "I've been through worse."

"I feel like there's a story there."

"We all have stories."

Ruarc's lips twisted. "Isn't that the fekking truth?"

Rordan chuckled as Ruarc took a long drink of whisky. "I have a feeling I may not be here that long."

"I noted that peculiar question sent your way. And the look that went with it. If I were you, I'd watch my back."

Rordan nodded and shifted to lean against the wall. The room was much smaller than the dining area, so the noise of conversation was louder. No one was close enough to overhear either him or Ruarc.

"I always do."

"Uh-oh," Ruarc said into his glass.

Rordan followed his gaze to find Dorcha headed their way. He steeled himself, waiting for whatever would happen. Except it wasn't Rordan the Fae wished to speak to.

Dorcha didn't even spare him a glance as he walked up and spoke to Ruarc. "I'd like you to begin helping Patrick and Casey immediately."

"As I said at dinner, I'll be happy to see what I can do. I didn't lie. A lot of things are in flux right now," Ruarc replied.

Dorcha smiled, but it didn't quite make it to his eyes. "It's very important that they get out of Dublin. Immediately."

"Everything I have is rented," Ruarc said.

Dorcha drew in a deep breath, his chest expanding. "Is it money you need?"

Rordan watched the two raptly. And he wasn't the only one. Fianna did, as well.

"Everything I have is rented," Ruarc repeated, anger beginning to show on his face and come through in his tone. "It has nothing to do with anything else."

"I'm sure you can kick someone out," Dorcha said.

Rordan raised his brows, taken aback by the cold remark.

"I could. If I wanted to," Ruarc stated. "But that isn't how I do business."

Dorcha's gaze narrowed. "It would be in your best interest to do exactly that."

Ruarc opened his mouth to reply. Rordan touched him on the arm in an effort to keep the Fae from reacting. However, the motion caused Dorcha's attention to turn to him. Rordan wasn't afraid of the Fae as so many others were. There was nothing anyone could blackmail him on or threaten him with. And while he wasn't immortal, it would take a lot for him to be killed. Being a Reaper put him in a unique position that none of the others had.

Most everyone at the manor fawned over Dorcha like he was their savior. Rordan didn't grovel to anyone, not even Death.

"Why are you here?" Dorcha demanded.

Out of the corner of his eye, Rordan saw Fianna move closer. "Like everyone else, I was curious to hear what you had to say. I came for the second meeting, and then you invited me to stay here."

"Why did you agree?"

"Why did you ask me?"

Dorcha glanced around to see if anyone was listening. "Someone is suspicious of you."

"So you invite me into your home?" Rordan asked with a quirked brow, not believing a word of it. "That isn't the move I would've made."

Dorcha smiled and made a little noise in the back of his throat. "You're rough around the edges, Rordan. Perhaps you don't know what it means to be in the company of the aristocrats."

"I know exactly what it means, unfortunately."

"I think it's prudent that I get to know you better."

Rordan shrugged. "Ask anything you want."

"Who are you?" Dorcha asked immediately.

"I'm no one of importance, if that's what you mean."

"Where do you live?"

Rordan swirled the whisky in his glass before bringing it to his lips to drink. Only then did he say, "I move around a lot."

"And your family?"

"I've not seen them in thousands of years."

"Where are they?"

Rordan finished his whisky and set the glass on the table next to him. He looked into Dorcha's eyes and said, "I don't know, and I don't care. If you grill all potential members like this, then you might want to rethink that strategy. I'm not asking about your past or your family. Maybe I should."

Dorcha jerked as if struck.

"I think I'll call it a night," Rordan said and walked out before he did something he'd later regret.

Too much rode on him getting intel for him to be an idiot. So many smartass remarks nearly spilled from his mouth, but he managed to keep them to himself. That was a huge victory. But he had to get away from Dorcha and balance the chaos within him if he were to continue his mission. Death and the other Reapers were counting on him to be successful.

His steps took him out of the manor and down the path he'd used earlier. He didn't stop until he stood before the lough. The water was like glass with the moonlight shimmering upon it. The sounds of the night surrounded him, and he drew in a deep breath before releasing it. Instantly, he was calmer.

It wasn't just Dorcha that had gotten under his skin. It was the manor, the opulence, the extravagance. The self-indulged, egotistical twats. He hated all of it because it took him back to his childhood and the years that had shaped him into something he hadn't recognized. It had gotten so bad that he hadn't been able to look at himself in the mirror.

To this day, he didn't know why Death had given him a second chance and made the offer for him to join the ranks of the Reapers. From the moment he'd taken her offer, he'd been a better Fae, an honorable one who never let his brethren down.

But no matter how much he told himself that, the past came bubbling up. He closed his eyes and fisted his hands. The past couldn't hurt him now. That didn't stop the memories from replaying like a movie in his head. He tried to halt them, attempted to think of something else, but they wouldn't shut off.

"They're just memories. The past," he whispered.

CHAPTER EIGHT

After Rordan departed, Fianna stalked over to her brother. Ruarc quickly excused himself, leaving the two of them alone. She glared at Dorcha and asked, "What the hell was that?"

"I've a right to ask such questions."

"Since when? You've never cared about anyone's past before. And who is suspicious of him? Because it sure isn't me."

Dorcha grabbed her arm, his fingers biting into her flesh as he pulled her behind a potted plant to shield them from prying eyes. "Lower your damn voice."

"What is wrong with you?" She jerked her arm out of his grasp and looked him up and down. "You're acting strange."

"It doesn't matter who is suspicious. Someone is."

"Since I'm your head of security, I should know about all threats. None has been brought to my attention, nor have I seen anything that would raise suspicion regarding Ruarc or Rordan. You need to tell me what's going on right now."

Dorcha snorted loudly. "I don't have to tell you anything. You're head of security because Da wanted to give you a job to make you feel like you were part of this family. And that is the only thing you can do."

"Is that right?" she asked, shocked, hurt, and angry at his words.

"I saw you and Rordan tonight."

She blinked, taken aback. "Excuse me?"

"I saw the two of you talking."

She shrugged, shaking her head. "So? I talked to everyone here."

"But he was *looking* at you."

"If you remember, I'm the one who didn't want to come to this thing. You said Da told me I had to, so you can't blame any of this on me. I did as requested."

Dorcha moved closer, crowding her. "Do I really need to remind you of your past? The one you keep swearing is behind you. Do I really need to show you pictures? Do I need to compare you and our mother again?"

"No," she bit out.

"Maybe it's time you go back in the box."

It took all of her self-control not to lash out at her brother with a physical punch followed by a wallop of magic that would land him on his arse. "I've not seen you like this since those times."

"Oh, don't try that, dear little sister. One call to Da, and you won't see daylight for the next five hundred years." He pointed his finger at her, jabbing it into her shoulder. "One. Call." He straightened and took a step back. "Do we understand each other?"

Yeah, she really wanted to kick him in the balls. "Perfectly," she replied icily.

He plastered a smile on his face and walked back to their guests, talking loudly. Fianna, however, was shaken. This was the Dorcha she'd known when they were growing up. She'd thought they were past all of that, but apparently, she had been wrong. What frightened her the most was that she would lose her freedom again if she didn't do exactly what he wanted. And that couldn't happen.

She teleported outside to get away from everyone. And to look for Rordan. She had seen him exit the manor. He wasn't near the house, so she started down the trail to the back of the property. She wasn't surprised to find him by the lough.

As she walked closer, she realized that he stood rigid, his eyes closed, and his hands fisted. Fianna was cautious as she neared. She didn't want to startle him, but at the same time, he looked to be in pain. The fact that she had sought him out should be enough to send her straight to her room, particularly because of Dorcha's recent threat.

But she stayed.

In the state he was in, being surprised could lead him to react defensively. Instead of calling his name, she tossed a stick into the water to alert him that he was no longer alone. Rordan's eyes snapped open. "I'm sorry," she said.

He turned his head to her, their eyes meeting. "For what?"

"My brother."

Rordan swung his gaze back to the water. "You don't need to apologize for him."

"He's normally not like this."

As she spoke, Rordan's hands unclenched, and he visibly relaxed. If she were smart, she would leave him with his thoughts. Yet the seconds passed as she remained. It was folly, but even knowing that, she couldn't get her feet to move. It wasn't as if she were doing anything. All they were doing was talking.

They just happened to be alone.

In the dark.

Rordan's intense gaze speared her. Not even the darkness could hide the desire she saw there. Awareness stole over her. The nerve endings along her skin prickled, her blood heated. It had been so long since she had felt this. If Rordan came towards her, she wouldn't push him away. A side of her silently begged him to approach. When he shifted to face her, she let out a relieved sigh.

"Why are you defending him?" Rordan asked.

Fianna kicked off her shoes to let her bare feet feel the earth. "He's my brother, family. Doesn't everyone defend their family?"

"No."

One simple word. But with a wealth of meaning and emotion behind it. Fianna wanted to ask him what he meant but thought better of it. She shrugged as she dug her toes into the ground. "Dorcha and my father are all I have."

"You have much more than that. Look around you," Rordan told her as he swept his arm wide. "Not only are you a strong, independent female who can handle herself, but you've trained a number of guards who work for you."

She cocked her head at him, surprise rushing through her. "How do you know all of that?"

"I asked," he replied with a grin.

She couldn't help but smile.

"The security here is very good, and all of that is because of you. Your guards respect you, and that isn't always an easy thing to accomplish. You don't need to stay here."

And just like that, her smile was wiped away. "Why would you say that?"

"Family is nice to have. Up until they try to control you. That's when you need to take a hard look at yourself and figure out if you really need them, or if they need you."

She frowned at his words. "It sounds like you've had a difficult time with your family. And for that, I'm sorry. But mine is different. They were there for me when no one else was. They…." She stopped, shocked that she had been about to tell him the worst part of her life. Those words had never even come close to passing her lips, but for some reason, she had almost told someone she barely knew.

"They what?" he pressed.

Fianna pressed her lips together and shook her head. "It doesn't matter. They're my family, and I will always stand by them. It's too bad you don't have that kind of relationship with yours."

"I'm incredibly close with my family. I would do anything for them, and they for me. The only difference is, they aren't blood."

Before she could think of a reply to that, he kept talking.

"What I don't understand is you. You're smart, beautiful, and a true warrior. You shouldn't be alone."

She jerked back, offended. "Do you think a female isn't complete unless she's paired with someone?"

"I don't. I just wanted to see your reaction."

Fianna blew out a frustrated breath and looked at the water. "I came out here because of how Dorcha treated you. I'm beginning to regret that."

"He's very protective of you. That could either be because he's making sure no one oversteps if you're already spoken for, or...."

When he didn't finish, she slid her gaze to him and prompted, "Or?"

"He wants you for himself."

Fianna started laughing. "You've no idea what you're talking about."

"I didn't say he did. I said it was a possibility," Rordan said.

Without meaning to, Fianna thought about Dorcha's comment inside the manor about someone being suspicious of Rordan. She recalled how subdued he had been at the first meeting, as well as the second. He wasn't as enthusiastic as the others who stayed at the manor. She had thought that might be because of his personality. But now, she had to wonder if there was something more.

"Why are you here?" she demanded.

He quirked a brow and removed his jacket as he said, "You heard my answer to Dorcha. It hasn't changed."

"If you believe in what my brother has been sharing, what Fae from all over the globe come to hear him speak about, then you would've given that as your answer."

Rordan carefully folded the jacket in half and draped it over his left arm. "That's the reason I came to the first and second meetings. I'm here tonight, staying in the manor, because I was invited."

They stared at each other for a long moment, the silence broken only by the sounds of the night. Fianna was about to leave when Rordan sighed loudly.

"Why did your brother invite me?"

Fianna swallowed, not at all prepared to answer such a question. "I don't know. He's never done anything like that before."

Rordan walked to her, stopping a few feet in front of her. "The fact he needs security should give you some concern. Also, you might want to make sure you have the same measures in place for yourself."

"Me?" she asked in shock.

"You're his sister. If someone wants to get to him, they could take you and force his hand."

Fianna knew such a play would get nothing from either Dorcha or their father, but she kept that tidbit to herself.

"Be safe, Fianna."

He strode past her. Their talk hadn't been great, but she didn't want him to leave. She turned around. As she searched for something to say that would stop him, she couldn't come up with anything. So, she watched him fade into the darkness.

It was for the best. Fianna told herself that over and over. Even though she knew it was the truth, she still didn't like it. Nor did she particularly care for the fact that she had wanted him to stay and keep talking, despite their odd conversation.

She walked to the water, stood in the spot Rordan had been, and looked at the lough. Her thoughts were on Rordan and the mystery that seemed to surround him. He didn't appear fervent about Dorcha's plan, though just because Rordan wasn't jumping up and down didn't mean he wasn't in agreement. Why then did Dorcha put him under such close scrutiny? Surely, it couldn't be as Rordan suggested?

When they were kids growing up, she and Dorcha had hated each other, but she just assumed that's how siblings were. Once their mother was gone, Dorcha modeled himself after their father as she went down a very dark, incredibly lonely road. Only after her father stepped in and forced her to reevaluate her life did she see what she had become.

During that horrendous time, the only one she had spoken to was her father. If Dorcha had been there, she hadn't seen him. Dorcha approached her only after she had shaken off her old life for good. Though they were siblings, they were also strangers. With both her and Dorcha once more living with their father, they began learning about each other and eventually became friends.

Until tonight. She had seen the old hatred in his eyes. Maybe he was just having a bad night. She would talk to him tomorrow and see how he acted.

"Am I interrupting?"

She jerked her head to the side to see Ruarc smiling at her. She returned it and said, "Not at all."

"I wasn't going to bother you since you looked as if you were mulling something important over, but I wanted to see if you were all right."

"Of course. Why wouldn't I be?"

Ruarc stared blankly at her for a moment, then walked a few steps closer. "I saw what he did to you. How Dorcha grabbed you."

"It was just a row between siblings."

"I don't agree with that. That kind of grabbing leads to more physical abuse."

Fianna licked her lips and faced him. "I appreciate your concern. I really do. But it was just a spat. Besides, Dorcha knows better than to hit me. I'd have him unconscious in seconds."

"And what is your excuse for how he treated Rordan? And me?"

"I don't have one. I'm not privy to my brother's thoughts. I don't know what someone might have told him."

Ruarc nodded solemnly. "My irritation isn't aimed at you. I shouldn't have asked you that question. I was looking for Rordan. Have you seen him?"

"He was here a few moments ago. He headed back to the manor."

"Thanks," Ruarc said and started to turn away.

Fianna reached out and put a hand on his arm to stop him. "Dorcha is having an off night. This isn't him. You know that."

"I don't take kindly to threats. From anyone."

She frowned as she took in his pinched lips that showcased his anger. "A good night's sleep is all anyone needs. You'll see. It'll be fine in the morning."

Ruarc bowed his head in response, then walked away. Fianna watched him, wondering why her brother had gone after both Rordan and Ruarc. There had to be something there, and she was going to find out what it was.

Fianna walked to her shoes and grabbed them before snapping her fingers, replacing the white jumpsuit with her usual black attire. Then she made the rounds of the estate as her conversation with Rordan went through her mind over and over again.

CHAPTER NINE

He'd had a chance to get some real information from Fianna, and instead, he'd let his anger boil over from his run-in with Dorcha. Rordan couldn't believe he had been so stupid. Now, he would have to work extra hard to mend what he had fractured.

She had come to *him*. Fianna had sought him out. He still could hardly believe it. It certainly wasn't something he'd expected her to do. He wanted to believe it was because she had wished to talk to him, but Rordan couldn't help but wonder if Dorcha had sent her. With the way Fianna had spoken of their family, she'd let it be known that she would do anything and everything for them.

Rordan had seen the destruction the Others could cause. He'd seen the havoc they wrought on not just the Dragon Kings but also the Fae, Druids, and even the mortals. That was why he had such a difficult time understanding why anyone would go down that path again. It all came down to ego and power.

He thought about veiling himself and jumping into Dorcha's office. The Fae likely had spells to alert him of anyone doing just that. Not to mention, Dorcha would expect someone to try something like that, so there was probably nothing there to find.

If he were to get information, then Rordan needed to go about it another way. After tonight and the confrontation, he wasn't sure Dorcha would allow him into whatever organization he was putting together. The sad part was that everyone who came to the meetings believed that Dorcha would help unify the Fae.

But Rordan knew the truth. It was all a front for the Others. Those who bought into Dorcha's eloquent speeches and charm would find themselves involved in something that could potentially be devastating to the Fae.

Rordan glanced around the dense woods as he slowed his pace. He veiled himself in case others were watching. After so many centuries as a Reaper, he was used to living in the shadows, and he didn't like being out in the open as he was. He halted and moved off the path to simply listen to nature. He had no wish to return to his room, and he couldn't leave Moorehall. Not yet, anyway. In order to finish his mission, he had to forget about his anger, as well as his mounting attraction to Fianna.

Just thinking about her brought her image to mind. He liked her hair down—the thick strands straight and glossy, adding an air of sophistication. She was a beauty in her shapeless, black guard attire, but she had been exquisite tonight in white. She had, quite literally, stolen his breath when he'd seen her walk into the dining room.

Ruarc had known what his reaction would be, too, because the Fae had been watching him the entire time. Rordan knew that he would've pursued Fianna had he met her in another life. Her quiet strength called to him. She had seen a lot in her years, but she had also overcome it.

Rordan thought about asking Death for Fianna's background

but decided against it. It wasn't essential to know about the siblings to discern what they were doing. What he needed to uncover was how Dorcha was connected to the Others.

The sound of voices drew his attention. He swung his head around, trying to determine their location. It wasn't at the lake, nor near the manor. They sounded much deeper in the woods. When Rordan heard Dorcha's voice, he used magic to remove his suit and replace it with jeans, a tee, and his favorite boots. Then he veiled himself and began to move through the forest quietly. No one could see him, but they *could* hear him if he wasn't careful.

Being able to stay veiled for as long as he wanted was just one of the perks of being a Reaper. Rordan called his knives to him, placing them all over his body. He pulled one from the strap that now lay across his chest and softly closed his fingers around the handle.

He finally found Dorcha and the four Fae males some distance from the manor. Two of the newcomers were Dark, and the other two were Light Fae. Without needing to listen to any words, Rordan could tell that Dorcha was frightened of them. Rordan had to admit, the four were intense individuals. Not just in their manner of all-black attire but in the way they held themselves. As if they feared nothing.

One Light and one Dark stood together closest to Dorcha as they listened to him. The other Light and Dark stood a couple of steps behind their counterparts. Rordan's gaze moved to who appeared to be the leaders of the four. He studied the Dark, the sides of his head shaved and a pompadour style on top that looked much better than Dorcha's.

Something about these Fae made Rordan think of when Dubhan and Kyra had run into a mixed group of Fae who had then attempted to attack them. They believed that the group was an offshoot of the Others. Dubhan and Cathal had both said the group was very powerful. These four certainly fit that description.

"Do you have what we requested?" the Dark demanded.

"I'm almost certain, but I need more time," Dorcha told them. "Things are coming together. I can't rush any of it."

"We've given you more than enough time," the Light Fae stated in a cold voice. His black hair was long and loose, his clothes high quality.

Dorcha shifted nervously. "I've only recently found it. The last one turned out not to be what you sought. I want to make sure this time."

The lead Dark turned his head and looked directly at Rordan. Rordan might be veiled, but he knew better than to move. He didn't know how the Dark knew he was there, but it was obvious that the Fae did. The more Rordan watched them, the more he suspected the group's powers might be close to those of a Reaper.

"Please," Dorcha begged.

The Dark swung his head back to Dorcha. "Have you gotten Patrick and Casey settled yet?"

"I'm working on it," Dorcha answered.

The Dark just stared. It was the Light who said, "Need I remind you what we're holding?"

Dorcha shook his head. "I'm well aware what you have."

"We'll be back in two nights. You'd better have what we seek by then," the Light stated.

Three of the Fae teleported out, but the lead Dark remained, his gaze once more focused in Rordan's direction. Several tense seconds passed as Rordan waited to see if the Dark would throw magic to uncover whether someone was veiled. Finally, he left. Rordan watched as Dorcha ran a hand down his face to wipe away the sweat and then sighed loudly. After a couple of minutes to compose himself, Dorcha plastered on a smile and started back toward the manor.

Rordan jumped to the small cottage he'd been renting and called Dubhan's name. The Reaper didn't take long to appear. The moment he did, Rordan asked, "Tell me again about the group of Fae you and Kyra ran across when you went to visit Max."

Dubhan's brows snapped together, and his red eyes filled with concern. "There were eight of them. Four Light, four Dark. But there seemed to be a leader for both."

"Did the Light have long hair?"

Dubhan thought a moment, then nodded. "Aye. The one in charge of the Dark had the sides of his hair trimmed very close and—"

"A pompadour hairstyle," Rordan finished.

"You found them."

Rordan briefly raised his brows. "It looks as if I did."

"So Dorcha is involved in this new group of Others as Erith suspected."

"I don't know specifics yet, but I'm going to find out."

Dubhan's red eyes grew intense. "You need to be careful. These Others are powerful."

"I know. I was veiled, but the lead Dark still kept looking my way."

"If they discover a Reaper is here, they'll go straight for you."

"That is if they know about Reapers," Rordan replied.

Dubhan snorted loudly. "Always expect them to know. It's better that way. You shouldn't be on this mission alone. You need someone to watch your back. The others can handle their search for Xaneth. I'm going to stay with you."

"If I need help, I'll give a shout. I can handle this. I'm just gathering information."

Dubhan bowed his head. "Watch your back, brother."

After Dubhan left, Rordan sat in his cottage for another few minutes before teleporting to the manor.

Dubhan jumped back to Barcelona, where the Reapers were gathered. Eoghan took one look at him and motioned him over.

"What happened?" the leader asked.

Dubhan ran a hand down his face. "The same Others Kyra and I ran into showed up at Moorehall."

Eoghan's quicksilver eyes briefly flared. "Erith was right, then. Dorcha and that family are involved with the Others. What else did Rordan tell you?"

"Nothing. I told him I'd remain and watch his back, but he said he could handle the mission. This group he's looking into is formidable."

"Rordan is undercover, which means we can't pop in or have him come to us. If he gets into a bind, he'll let us know."

Dubhan shook his head. "That group knew Kyra and I were there. And they sensed Rordan tonight. If they suspect a Reaper is near, they'll hunt him."

"You're speculating that they know about the Reapers."

"I'd rather not underestimate them. The Others knew of us. If this group is an offshoot of them—or worse, the same group with different members—then they know."

Eoghan flattened his lips as he nodded. "Good point. I'll speak to Erith and Cael."

"Xaneth?" Dubhan asked.

Eoghan blew out a deep breath. "Nothing. Yet."

"We'll find him."

"I'm not sure what state he'll be in when we do. We're assuming he left Usaeil's house on his own. All we could discern for certain was that he had been there."

"He was there, and he left," Aisling stated as she walked past.

Dubhan watched her. She was the first female Reaper, but to the rest of them, she was a sister.

"She'll be fine," Eoghan said, referring to Aisling. Then he slapped Dubhan on the shoulder and teleported out.

"Well?"

Borgar crossed his arms over his chest as he looked at his Light counterpart, Hemming, dressed in his all-white ensemble. It made him want to gag. "Someone was there."

"A Reaper?" Hemming asked.

"They were veiled."

Hemming's nostrils flared. "We could've taken him right then. A single blast of magic would have revealed them. You know this."

Borgar shook his head. "If it was a Reaper, they would've come at us."

"Or they were spying."

"You're the one who believes the way to the Reapers is through Dorcha's meetings. I think it's shite."

Hemming rolled his eyes. "Yes, I know perfectly well what you think."

"If we were the ones making decisions, nothing would get done because I believe your ideas are shite, and you think the same of mine."

"Definitely," Hemming stated emphatically.

Borgar inhaled a sharp breath and released it. "We put the pressure on Dorcha. If there *is* a Reaper at Moorehall, he'll show up in two nights."

"The beginning of the end of them," Hemming said with a smile.

CHAPTER TEN

When Fianna looked in the mirror the next morning, she saw the same face as always staring back at her. But something was different. She couldn't put her finger on what, but it was there.

She decided to ignore it and go about her day as she always did. When she left her room, she stopped in the corridor and listened to the sounds of the manor. Muffled voices from the stairway reached her. It was the back stairs, which meant it was the kitchen staff and the guards, getting their breakfast.

She turned to the main stairway then walked closer to it and leaned against the railing to peer down. Faint voices reached her from the dining room. She had no desire to talk to anyone from the previous night. Well, except for maybe Rordan.

She twisted her lips. Perhaps not. She had done her duty the night before. She had dressed as expected and sat through a long meal, then stood around making idle—if insipid—conversation with people who only wanted to speak with her because she was Dorcha's sister. It didn't matter what Dorcha or her father said. She wouldn't do that again. It wasn't as if they had Dorcha training with her for battle. Why should she be a part of his world?

Fianna turned to retrace her steps and ascended the back stairs. She walked past Dorcha's room and heard something within. Since he was always there for his guests, she assumed he was downstairs. Fianna went to his door and pressed her ear close. She heard a voice that wasn't her brother's, so she opened the door, thinking she would find one of the guests snooping in his room.

Instead, she found her brother still in his clothes from the night before, looking as if he hadn't rested at all. He had dark circles under his eyes, his shirt was half-untucked, and his hair was in disarray.

"What the bloody hell?" he demanded when he saw her.

She blinked and spotted Lewis in the room, but Dorcha moved to block her view. "I thought I heard someone. I came to make sure—"

"Knock next time," Dorcha barked, his face contorted with fury.

She started to turn away when he suddenly grabbed her arm. Fianna winced as he dug his fingers in on almost the exact spot as the night before.

"Wait. Wait," he said, his voice calmer. He smiled at her. "I'm sorry. It's been a long night."

"So I see."

"I need your help."

She grabbed his wrist and tugged it away from her arm. "What do you need?"

"Make sure that Ruarc finds Patrick and Casey houses."

"You crossed a line with Ruarc last night. I don't think he's going to help."

"That's why you must convince him," Dorcha insisted.

Fianna looked into eyes that pleaded with her. It was good to be needed by her family, and whenever they came to her like this, she could never say no. And they knew that. "I'll give it a shot, but I'm not promising anything."

"Thank you."

He appeared close to tears, which was not like her brother at all. "What is going on? And don't tell me you're fine because we both know you aren't."

Dorcha dropped his head into his hands, his shoulders shaking. Fianna glanced left then right down the hall to make sure no one saw them before backing him into the room and closing the door behind her. She ignored Lewis, who had turned away from them. She would find out why he was in her brother's room later.

"Dorcha?"

He lifted his head and wiped at his red-rimmed eyes. "We're in trouble. Big trouble. And if we don't get this right, they're going to kill Da."

"This isn't the time for jests," she said and crossed her arms over her chest.

"I'm not joking."

She gazed deep into Dorcha's eyes and comprehended that he was telling the truth. "Da is secreted away. No one knows where he is."

"They found him."

"They who?"

Dorcha shook his head. "You don't want to know. All that matters is that they have Da."

"What do we need to do to get him back?"

"I need to get certain people to join our cause."

She shrugged, unsure why that was a difficult thing. "Anyone who listens to your words understands how important your mission is. You have hundreds trying to get into the organization."

Dorcha started to laugh. He turned away, disgust on his face. "Right."

"What am I missing?"

"Everything."

She threw up her hands. "How can I help if you won't tell me everything?"

"You're useless. Get out," he ordered.

Fianna stared at his back, hoping he'd say something else. Finally, she left his room and went in search of Ruarc. Maybe if she got him to do as Dorcha wanted, her brother would reveal whatever it was he was keeping secret. How could she fully help her family if they kept things from her?

She searched the entire manor as well as the grounds and couldn't locate Ruarc. So, she looked for Rordan. She hoped the two of them might be together since they seemed to have struck up a friendship. She was surprised to find him at the training area.

She watched as he spoke to a couple of her guards. He was at ease, smiling, even chuckled on a couple of occasions. Maybe the darkness, as well as the odd way her brother had acted at the dinner, had caused her to read more into her conversation with Rordan than what had actually been.

Suddenly, he turned, and their gazes met. He bowed his head. She lifted a hand in acknowledgement and started toward him. He broke away from the guards and met her halfway.

"I hope your offer to spar still stands," he said.

"Of course."

His brows briefly drew together. "I'd like to apologize for last night. I was in a foul mood, and I shouldn't have taken it out on you."

"The entire night was peculiar. Let's forget it ever happened," she offered.

"I'd like that."

"You haven't seen Ruarc, have you?"

The frown was back, more pronounced this time. "Actually, I haven't."

"He looked for you last night not long after you returned to the manor. I'd hoped to check on him this morning." She left out exactly what she wanted.

"He might be tending to business," Rordan offered.

Fianna hoped that was the case. One way or another, she had to track him down and persuade him to help her and Dorcha.

"Care to spar with me?"

She couldn't stop the smile. "Absolutely."

The minute she and Rordan stepped into the training ring, the others stopped their sparring and moved to the side. She noted the way several of the guards watched Rordan with excitement. For all she knew, he had already sparred with some of them. She was too seasoned to allow their expressions to mix up her emotions.

She and Rordan faced each other. She took up a defensive position with her knees bent and her left leg forward, her weight evenly distributed. Her arms were up near her face, hands fisted. With this pose, she could punch with her fists, or she could call up magic.

Rordan grinned at her. He stood casually as if waiting for her to make the first move. The next thing she knew, he attacked. He was fast—faster than anyone she had ever sparred with before. She blocked several of his moves, but he got in even more hits. What angered her was that she knew he was pulling his punches.

They broke apart, and to her dismay, she found herself winded. "Don't hold back."

When they clashed again, she ended up on her back. She wasn't even sure what move he had used, but she quickly wrapped her legs around his and rolled, taking him down, as well. She kicked up to her feet and smiled down at him.

Rordan grinned as he stood and dusted himself off. "Nice job."

"Shall we continue this, or would you like to try staves or perhaps swords?"

Without hesitation, he reached for a staff. Fianna got one, as well. This time, she attacked first. She got the first strike, but he quickly matched her. They went back and forth for a while until sweat ran down both their faces. It wasn't until he used the staff to knock her off her feet that he squatted beside her and held out his hand.

"Swords?" he asked.

She took his hand with a laugh as he helped her to her feet. "Of course."

Fianna forgot about the turmoil of last night. She forgot about Dorcha's unusual behavior. She forgot that her father was missing. She forgot everything but Rordan and the fun she was having.

Just by sparring with him, she had picked up a few new moves she hadn't seen before. Despite her telling him not to hold back, he continued to do so. He had been amazing with his hand-to-hand combat, as well as the staff, but it seemed his specialty was swords. Her father had been fastidious with sword training for both her and Dorcha, so she knew how important it could be to some families— particularly the nobility.

The way Rordan used the blade as an extension of his body, the ease with which he deflected blows and parried, was some of the best she had ever witnessed. And she had seen quite a lot. The more she saw of Rordan, the more she began to believe that he belonged to some noble family.

Then, with a quick twist of his wrist, he caught her off balance and caused her sword to go flying out of her hand, landing on the ground and effectively ending their sparring session. The air erupted with cheers. She couldn't remember the last time anyone had beaten her so soundly.

"That was impressive," she told him.

He grinned, shrugging indifferently. "It comes in handy on occasion."

"Can I hire you as one of my guards?"

His silver eyes darkened with blatant desire. As quickly as the emotion appeared, it vanished. "Sadly, no."

"Let me know if you ever change your mind."

"I will."

She smoothed hair that had come loose from her ponytail back from her face. "If you ever want to do this again, I'm always game."

"I'll remember that."

With the training over, the worries of before came rushing back. She wanted to contact her father to see if he really had been taken. Dorcha had been acting so weird, she wasn't certain if he spoke truthfully. Then there was the fact that he was clearly keeping something from her.

"I'd like to look for Ruarc, as well. Why don't we pair up?" Rordan offered.

Fianna hesitated because she already liked being around him too much. The demons of her past were always right there, waiting to get out and destroy everything once more. On the other hand, she really needed to locate Ruarc, and two pairs of eyes were always better than one.

"I'd like that," she said. "I've already searched the manor and grounds."

"We can go to his house on the island."

Fianna nodded. "Let me tell the guards to keep an eye out for him."

After she'd spoken to her people, she glanced down at her attire. It was one thing to wear her security garb at the manor, but she would stand out walking the streets. She rarely left Dorcha's side, so there was no need for her to wear much of anything else. Fianna decided to change her clothes, and with a thought, jeans, a sleeveless beige sweater, and sandals relaced the boxy, black uniform.

Rordan quirked a brow when he saw her. "I'm not sure if I like this outfit or the white one from last night better."

She smiled, her stomach quivering as if a thousand butterflies had taken flight. No one ever spoke about her clothes, so to have compliments two days in a row was something different. And it made her want to seriously consider rethinking some things about her life.

"Do you know where he lives?" Rordan asked.

She nodded and put her hand on his arm, jumping them to the location. Only after they had arrived at Ruarc's house did she realize she hadn't notified Dorcha of where she was going—or who she was with. After the way he'd forced her to the dinner and had spoken to her earlier, this was her revenge.

Fianna noted that Rordan was looking at her peculiarly. She wiped the frown from her face and smiled. "Just thinking."

Together, they walked to the door of the house. It was a nice place with plenty of land between Ruarc and the neighbors on either side of him.

Rordan knocked on the door, but no one answered. "Ruarc? It's Rordan."

Not even that produced the Fae.

"Maybe he's out back," Fianna offered.

They walked to the back of the house and saw the stunning meadow covered in wildflowers. But there was still no sign of Ruarc.

"Ruarc," Rordan called.

No matter where the Fae was, he would hear Rordan say his name and come to him. The minutes ticked by without Ruarc's appearance.

"I don't have a good feeling about this," Rordan said.

Neither did she. "He was upset when I saw him last night. Said he wasn't going to allow anyone to blackmail him into doing anything."

Rordan glanced at her and called Ruarc's name again. Then, Rordan turned to her. "Why is it so important that Ruarc find those two Fae places to live? Why can't they do it themselves? Or find someone else?"

"I don't know," she said. "This morning, Dorcha asked me to find Ruarc and convince him to help us."

"Why Ruarc, specifically?" Rordan pushed.

Fianna blew out a breath. "My father did a favor for Ruarc's family once. As payment, Ruarc has made sure to get Dorcha prime locations for his meetings. I think Dorcha wants to keep cashing in on that debt, but Ruarc has done more than enough."

"How so?"

"We don't pay for the time we spend in homes such as Moorehall."

Rordan nodded slowly. "I see. What's so important about tomorrow night?"

She frowned as she shrugged. "Nothing. Other than it's the last meeting to see who Dorcha brings into the fold."

"Why does he do that? Seems to me, if he wants the support of all, he should be willing to accept anyone who wants to give it. Why go through the meetings and be so selective?" Rordan asked.

It was a question she had asked once, as well. Her da and Dorcha hadn't bothered to answer. "You would have to ask Dorcha."

"I think I will."

CHAPTER ELEVEN

Worry for Ruarc filled Rordan. All he had to do was go to Death and have her locate him, but he didn't want to do that in case it alerted the Others. There was a good chance Ruarc had gotten away. If that were the case, it would be better if Rordan left him alone. Yet, the memory of the four Fae speaking to Dorcha the previous night left him uneasy.

"You're not telling me something."

Rordan looked into Fianna's silver eyes. She searched his gaze, waiting for him to answer. But he couldn't. She had admitted that she would do anything for her family. He had to assume that she was part of everything Dorcha was doing—even if Rordan wished otherwise. However, he knew better than anyone that wishing something away didn't make it so.

Given the determination settling over her face, Rordan had to come up with something to say. So, he told her something as close to the truth as he could. "I'm troubled about Ruarc."

"Are you two close? I got the impression you had just met."

"We did," Rordan admitted. "But we get on well."

Fianna's lips pressed together. "And both of you were singled out by Dorcha last night."

Rordan didn't bother to respond to the statement. He watched Fianna carefully, noting the frustration she fought to keep hidden. It bubbled over anyway. He thought about asking her about it, but he wouldn't believe anything she said, no matter how she answered. She was with Dorcha, after all.

And that bothered him. There was no other way to say it. Rordan was aware that it was because he was attracted to her. Hell, even standing with her now challenged him not to touch her, to pull her against him, to lower his head to her lips. They were alone, something that wouldn't happen while at Moorehall. Sure, he'd had a few moments with her last night by the lough, but with the way Dorcha watched over her, that likely wouldn't happen again. If he were ever going to know the taste of her kiss, now was the moment.

Rordan let it pass him by.

"What now?" Fianna asked.

"I don't know."

Her eyes narrowed slightly. "I have to find Ruarc."

"Because those two Fae need to move? Plenty of others can help them find something."

Fianna hastily looked away. Rordan stared at her intently. Obviously, there was much more to Ruarc than he'd first thought.

"Now look who isn't sharing," he stated. When she didn't look at him, much less answer, Rordan thought out loud. "Ruarc has many holdings all over Ireland—and most likely the world. Your family did a favor for his, putting him in debt to yours. In return, he procured locations for Dorcha to have his meetings, gathering particular kinds of people to his…organization."

"A dream my father had that Dorcha is fulfilling," Fianna replied.

Rordan raised a brow. "And you aren't?"

"I'm with him, aren't I?"

It wasn't an answer, and they both knew it. Rordan let it go for now. "Ruarc wasn't sure why Dorcha invited him to stay at the manor. Dorcha singled out Ruarc at the dinner table so that everyone could hear his request, which then put Ruarc in a tenuous position. Chiefly because he said he couldn't help the two Fae. And Dorcha wouldn't take no for an answer. What is so important about those two Fae? Why does it have to be Ruarc who helps them?"

Fianna shrugged, refusing to meet his gaze.

There were few options for why the two Fae were so important, and he knew it had nothing to do with nobility. He hadn't recognized the names, and from the looks of those around the table, none of the others did either. But Ruarc had.

"Who are Casey and Patrick?" he pressed Fianna.

She glanced at him and shrugged again. "Two associates of my brother."

"Not your family?"

"I've heard their names, but I've never met them."

"But you know who they are."

She turned her head and blew out a breath. "I need to get back to the manor."

"I'm not holding you here. You can leave anytime."

But she stayed, giving him hope that she might divulge some piece of information. After several silent moments, she looked at him. "Ruarc runs a good business. He's respected and highly sought out. However, there is another side to his business that he's been unable to extract himself from, and that is the many and various debts and favors his family owes."

"And those people come to him to call in favors or debt, just as your family did."

Fianna's nose wrinkled. "Precisely. I was never comfortable with it, but our family has had issues of our own—as I'm sure you know."

"I don't listen to gossip."

Her head tilted to the side as her brows drew together. "You may be the only Fae in existence."

"I highly doubt that."

"I don't," she replied with a bite to her tone. She drew in a deep breath. "You really don't know?"

He shook his head.

"You didn't find it odd that you never hear Dorcha use a surname?"

Rordan crossed his arms over his chest. "I don't use one. I don't give much credence to such things."

"Only someone who comes from a wealthy family would say such things."

"Is that right?"

She snorted softly as she nodded. "Oh, yes. After what you said last night, and then just now."

"So, what if I did?"

"You found your way without your family. I lost my way without mine."

He shot her a dubious look. "I don't believe that for a moment."

"Do you know my family's name?" she pressed.

"No."

"If you did, you might not be standing with me now, much less staying at Moorehall."

Rordan's arms dropped to his sides at her statement. "If that were the case, then I imagine few know who you are. I've not heard anyone ask for a surname."

"Family means everything to my father. He raised Dorcha and me by himself. He has always been outspoken regarding what he sees for the future of the Fae. And for that, people have made attempts on his life. It's why his location is only known to Dorcha and me. When the scandal happened, my brother and I were very young. Da took us away to raise away from gossip and hate, but he told us everything when we were old enough."

The shame in her eyes and bearing infuriated Rordan. "You shouldn't carry the weight of the past, especially when it had nothing to do with you. A father should never do such a thing to his children."

"Maybe not. He did the best he could on his own."

"And your mother?"

Fianna's gaze dropped to the ground as she sat there for a moment. "She is the reason my father had to take us away. She's the reason there was a scandal at all."

The more she talked, the more Rordan wanted to know her family name. He didn't like Dorcha, and he wasn't too keen on her father either. "What is your surname?"

"Who is your family?" she asked in response.

Rordan blinked, taken aback by her question. Although, he should've seen it coming. It didn't matter if he wanted to tell her or not. He couldn't.

"That's what I thought," she said when he remained silent.

"There are reasons I don't give you an answer."

Fianna smiled, but it didn't reach her eyes. "Same."

He needed to get them back on safer ground. "Is there anywhere else you can think of to look for Ruarc?"

"I didn't know him very well. I've only spoken to him a handful of times. Moorehall is the first place we've stayed where he's been around."

"Then how did Dorcha know which places to go?"

Fianna threw up her hands in defeat. "I don't know that either. Dorcha always told me where we were going."

"You're in charge of security. That means you should be told what location you will be visiting so you can go there first to scout it out for possible threats."

"Yes, well, my father had other ideas. He wanted me with Dorcha at all times."

Rordan frowned. "Did he really believe that Dorcha was in that kind of danger?"

"Yes, and no."

Flummoxed didn't even begin to describe Rordan the more he learned. "What does that mean?"

Fianna swallowed nervously, which was his first clue. In the times he had watched her and had been near her, the one thing he hadn't seen was anxiousness. Unflappable and calm, absolutely. This was something that had developed as she spoke about her family. The longer it went on, the worse she became. He had thought he'd turned the conversation, but in actuality, he'd brought it back around to the one thing she didn't want to talk about.

"It doesn't matter," he quickly said.

She briefly closed her eyes. When she opened them, her expression was resolute. "Yes, he knows that people could come after Dorcha as they have him. But I'm the other reason."

"You?" Rordan asked in shock.

Fianna tried to force a smile but didn't quite succeed. "I did some foolish things long ago. Dorcha makes sure I don't screw up again."

Rordan turned away and ran his hand down his face. He was, in turn, furious and stunned. Out of Fianna and Dorcha, Dorcha was the one who should be watched, not Fianna. Rordan might not know the cause, but he had witnessed the siblings enough to know which one was on the right path, and which wasn't.

He spun back to face her. "Do you tell Dorcha everywhere you go?"

She nodded slowly. "Well, usually. He was quite upset this morning and told me to find Ruarc. He's not in a good frame of mind. I decided it was better to come out here without telling him."

"What happens if you get back and he finds out?"

"Typically, I would have to face my father."

That got his attention. "What's different this time?"

She dropped her head back to look at the sky. Then threw out her hands and started pacing as she spoke, her annoyance growing with each word. "Dorcha said Da is gone, which makes no sense. No one but us knows where our father is. Dorcha is keeping something else from me, too. He was scared, something I've never seen in his eyes before. He wants me to find Ruarc, and I can't even do that."

Rordan reached out and grabbed her by the shoulders, halting her. He caught her gaze and held it. "Take a deep breath. It's going to be fine."

"It isn't, though. I can feel it. Something has changed. Da always made the decisions and communicated them through Dorcha, which kept things stable. Inviting guests to Moorehall and the dinner…they're things Da never would've agreed to."

"Do you think your father has been taken?"

"I don't know. Maybe? I don't talk to him. Dorcha does."

It was the first time Rordan saw a hint of vulnerability, and his need to protect roared to life. He had been in a similar situation before, and it had left lasting scars. Despite that, he still found himself wanting to help her—even though he knew it could very well be a trap.

Rordan dropped his arms and straightened. His palms tingled from touching her bare skin. He wanted so much to believe everything she said, but he couldn't. From his observations, as well as Ruarc's statement, Fianna kept to herself. She rarely spoke to anyone but the guards. Even Dorcha seemed hellbent on keeping her away from others.

"You said it was Dorcha's first dinner party."

Fianna nodded. "He's never accepted such invitations anywhere or held an event like that before last night."

"And you?"

Her brow furrowed as she jerked her head back. "What about me?"

"Do you attend such things?"

"Why would I? I'm security. My job is to stay in the background."

"Yet, last night, you were front and center."

She rolled her eyes and said flatly, "Against my will."

"Dorcha forced you?"

Fianna pulled a strand of hair from her eyelashes and tried to smooth it back with the others, but the breeze yanked it from her grasp. "He told me Da ordered it. I had no reason not to believe him. The one thing we don't do is disobey our father. Ever."

So far, what she was telling him lined up with everything he'd overheard last night between Dorcha and the four Fae.

"I need to know what's going on. And I…" She paused and searched his face.

He fisted his hands so he wouldn't touch her once more. "You what?" he pressed when she didn't continue.

"I don't know what to do without Da."

"You're very capable. You don't need anyone telling you what to do."

She glanced at Ruarc's house. "I should get back to Moorehall and let Dorcha know I can't find Ruarc."

Rordan gave her a smile and a nod. She was waiting for him to return with her, but he wasn't ready for that. He needed to digest what he'd learned. Once more, he was tempted to call Death and get the background on Fianna and her family. The fact that Ruarc seemed to have disappeared, and the Fae Others Kyra and Dubhan had encountered had shown up the previous night made him decide against it.

He was close to getting answers. What those answers would be, he couldn't begin to guess.

CHAPTER TWELVE

Fianna knocked on Dorcha's door for a second time. He didn't answer, so she combed the manor for him. She found her brother in the gardens, staring at the flowers. She approached him warily. He didn't notice her until she was upon him.

Dorcha jerked his head to her. "Don't sneak up on me."

"I didn't."

"You did. Tell me things with Ruarc went as planned."

She heard Rordan's parting words and squared her shoulders. "I can't find him."

"What?" her brother bellowed. "Are you that incompetent?"

The past few days had reminded her of her childhood, and she wasn't about to go through such an ordeal again. "He's not on the grounds, nor is he at his house. I called for him, but he didn't come."

"That fekker. He owes us," Dorcha said between clenched teeth, spittle flying.

"He's repaid his family's debt twice over. He doesn't owe us anything."

Dorcha glowered at her. "I'll decide when his debt is paid."

"That isn't how this works. Besides, you don't make the decisions."

"I do now that Da is gone."

She narrowed her eyes at him and took a step closer. "Is Da dead? Did you have something to do with him being taken?"

"Of course not."

She shot him a scathing look. "I'm beginning to have my doubts."

"You can get off that high horse. We're in this together."

"In what?" she demanded. "What is going on?"

"I've told you more than you need to know."

She wanted to push him, to make him tell her. But that wasn't how her brother worked. Fianna decided to try a different approach. "Fine. Good luck locating Ruarc," she said and turned to leave.

"Where the bloody hell do you think you're going? And what are you wearing?"

Fianna halted, rolling her eyes at her brother's predictability. She pivoted to face him. "They're clothes, and I'm going back to my duties."

"I need your help." His words were less a petition than a command.

"I'm not doing anything until you tell me everything."

Dorcha stared silently at her for a time. "Someone took Da. I don't know why."

"Do you know what they want?"

"They've not told me yet."

She blew out a breath, feeling better now that he had opened up to her. "We're going to need to find out. Did they tell you how they found Da?"

"I didn't ask."

"No, I wouldn't have either. Until they get back with you, we can't do anything, right? We just need to carry on as we have?"

"Yes."

Fianna nodded slowly as she suddenly had a thought. "What about Patrick and Casey needing a place? Do they have anything to do with any of this?"

"Why would you ask that?" he barked, his tone biting.

"Because you're focused on finding Ruarc, and you only want him to get Casey and Patrick places."

"If they were part of it, I would've told you," he snapped.

But Fianna wasn't so sure. It wouldn't do any good to argue. She had gotten Dorcha to say all that he had. Never before had she cause to doubt her brother's word, but she did now. She'd known that something was off since he invited the guests to the manor. Her lips parted as she was about to ask how long ago their father had been taken, but she decided against it at the last minute. She couldn't put her finger on why. Still, her instincts were always right, and she would follow them on this occasion.

Fianna left Dorcha in the same place she had found him. With her mind still turning over everything, she examined every room in the manor, including those occupied by guests. When she walked to Rordan's room, she hesitated before knocking on the door. She wasn't sure why he hadn't returned with her. She had told him things she hadn't told another soul, and it had been so easy. Talking to him about anything was easy. He made her want to open up and tell him everything.

Fianna rapped on the door. She waited several moments. When he didn't answer, she knocked again, this time saying his name. Still, there was no answer. She turned the knob and opened the door, pushing it wide without stepping inside.

"Rordan?" she called. "I'm searching rooms."

Like all the others she had inspected, Fianna left the door wide and just scanned the space. She didn't open any drawers or even the closet. She finished quickly, but she found herself staring at the bed, imagining him sleeping there. Images of naked skin, limbs tangled in the sheets, and bodies rubbing against each other flashed in her mind.

She squeezed her eyes closed to stop the picture show. Then, she hastily left the room and moved on to the next. Nothing was out of place. She stayed as far from the guests as she could—they were scattered throughout the estate.

Once finished, Fianna was on her way downstairs when she looked up and spotted Rordan a few steps below her. She smiled at the sight of him. His lips softened, causing her stomach to quiver once more. He started to say something when Ruben and Ayda came in with some others, their conversation shattering the moment.

Rordan nodded to her and moved to the other side of the stairs as he continued on. She thought about following him and sharing what she had found out, though she wasn't sure why she wanted to share such things with him. Maybe it was because he seemed to care. It might be because of the attraction she felt.

He's a temptation. You know what happens if you continue on like this.

Fianna descended the stairs and began her sweep of the grounds. Not only did she want the time alone, but she also didn't want to trust this to anyone else. She needed to see things with her own eyes. The estate was large, and she took advantage of being by herself. On the occasions that she ran into one of her guards, she merely nodded. They knew their duties. She didn't need to micromanage them. However, she took the opportunity to study them before they knew of her approach.

Vast swaths of land on the estate weren't guarded. There were only so many for the positions, and she'd opted to keep them closer to the manor. Being alone in the woods was freeing. Fianna hadn't told Dorcha where she had gone earlier—or with who—and he had no idea where she was now. When she told Rordan that Dorcha had to know where she was at all times, she heard for the first time how asinine that sounded. She was her own person. Had she made mistakes? Absolutely. Everyone did. But she wasn't that person anymore.

Regardless if they found her father or not, she wouldn't check in with Dorcha like a child to a parent any longer. Her discussion with Rordan had opened her eyes to a lot of things—things she should've seen much, much earlier. It was easy to fall into a pattern. To gradually accept things that became normal. But hearing herself had been mortifying.

She stopped next to a fallen tree and sat upon it. Her gaze took in the clothes she hadn't changed out of after returning from searching for Ruarc. If it hadn't been for Dorcha forcing her to attend the dinner, she wouldn't have remembered how she liked dressing up or wearing heels. She wouldn't have changed into jeans and the sweater that day. But he had pushed her into doing what he wanted, and in turn, she had been compelled to take a good, long look at her life.

And she didn't like what she saw.

How did any of her guards obey her or take her seriously when Dorcha ordered her about like a slave? Since their father gave Dorcha the commands, she didn't know for certain what Da said about her or to her. Everything was filtered through Dorcha. What she couldn't understand was why she hadn't questioned that fact earlier.

But she was questioning everything now.

She owed her family. They'd helped her up from rock-bottom. But that didn't mean they had control of her life. At first, she had needed the structure so she didn't relapse, but she was stronger now. She could be on her own. She had become complacent and had accepted what her da wanted without argument.

"Not any longer."

Fianna quite liked the new person emerging within her, and she knew that Rordan had played a huge role in it. He had asked questions of her that no one else had, and that was because she never spoke to anyone about her family—she rarely spoke to anyone at all. When she did, it was about training or security. There were no conversations, no stories of the past or hopes for the future.

She released a long breath. The future. She couldn't remember the last time she had thought about her future. Everything had been tied to her father's vision of what the Fae should be. Gratitude had put her in a position to aid him—and thereby Dorcha—in any way she could.

Fianna contemplated leaving. Going somewhere and doing… something. The problem was, she didn't know where she wanted to go. Actually, that wasn't true. She wanted to be where Rordan was. He was an enigma she yearned to figure out. But more than that, she liked that he made her feel at ease. His open acceptance of her was something new. He didn't force his opinions on her or tell her how she should dress or act.

She got to her feet and continued her walk. Thinking about Rordan wouldn't help the situation. He was an attraction that would only trip her up and send her spiraling into the person that had to be saved by her family. No matter how much she liked how he made her feel, she needed to stay away. That was easy enough since she wasn't at the manor. She wouldn't blame him if he left as Ruarc had.

Two people missing from the meeting wouldn't be horrible. As her thoughts drifted to the gatherings, she considered Rordan's questions. He was right. If her father and Dorcha wanted to unite the Fae, they should take anyone and everyone. Why wasn't that happening? Maybe it was time she found out.

The day waned as she traversed the estate from one end to the other. By the time she reached the far side of the lough, it was dark. The water lapped gently against the shore and looked too enticing to ignore. She noticed the smooth water disturbed by a ripple, and then another. She followed them until she found the source —Rordan.

He swam with sure, strong strokes and glided effortlessly through the water. Her heart started hammering. She should leave.

Right then, before he saw her. But she couldn't stop looking at the muscles in his arms and shoulders.

Suddenly, he stopped swimming and stood. He shook his head, spraying water and disheveling his hair. He wiped his face with his hands and turned—his gaze landing on her.

CHAPTER THIRTEEN

Rordan couldn't believe that Fianna was there. She was the reason he had quit swimming because he couldn't stop thinking about her. After running into her on the stairs, he hadn't seen her for the rest of the day. And he had looked for her.

"I'm disturbing you again," she said.

He slowly shook his head. "Never. You okay? I've not seen you since this morning."

"I've been walking the property."

"Looking for anything in particular?"

She scratched her neck. "I wanted to do an entire sweep of the estate, and I needed to do it on my own."

"You weren't the only one missing. The other guests have been looking for Dorcha."

"That's not like him."

Rordan swiped at another droplet of water running down his face. "I don't suppose you've run across Ruarc?"

"No. I was about to ask you the same thing."

"Sadly, I've not seen him."

She swallowed and glanced around. "Well, I, uh…I guess I'll head back."

"Don't go."

Her gaze jerked to his as she stood silently. Rordan wasn't sure what he was doing. He needed information for his mission, though he wasn't sure he'd get much—if anything—from Fianna. But she was Dorcha's sister. Then there was his ever-increasing yearning for her. He knew it was madness, pure idiocy, to tempt himself so.

The grass-covered mountains rising in the distance appeared like shadowed spectators in the darkness. Rordan had admired their beauty earlier, but now, he couldn't take his eyes off Fianna. She had remained in her jeans and sweater. He thought about how smooth and soft her skin had felt, and he desperately wanted to touch her again.

"All right," she murmured.

Rordan teleported to the beach, calling his clothes to him as he did. The pebbled shoreline crunched beneath his feet as he moved closer to her. "I just thought you might need someone to talk to."

"Do I look lonely?"

"You look like someone who has a lot on their mind."

She twisted her lips. "I realized something today. I am lonely. I'm surrounded by others, but I don't have any friends. I used to have some. Lots of them."

"Friends are good. Some you can count on, but not all."

Her eyes were filled with regret and doubt. "You're the first person I've talked to about anything in what feels like eons. I talk to Dorcha and my da, but it's always about what they have planned, and what they want me to do. I talk to the guards, giving instructions. No one ever asks me about me. Until you."

Whatever hope Rordan had of keeping a lid on his attraction was blown away with those two words.

Fianna laughed and looked down to kick at the rocks. "I'm thinking of who I am, who I was, and who I want to be."

"Did you decide?"

She met his eyes and shrugged, a smile on her lips. "I came to one conclusion, though."

"What was that?"

"That my father and brother use me as nothing more than a slave. They're so afraid I'm going to do something that one of them has to know my whereabouts at all times. And I was fine with that because it was the next step in helping me regain my life. Then it became the norm. So habitual, I didn't even comprehend what they had done. What I had allowed them to do."

"You are your own person. You can do whatever you want," he told her.

She looped her fingers in her belt loops and swung from side to side as she glanced at the sky. "That's not how things work with my family."

"It's how things work if that's what you want. What is it you want?"

"For someone to see *me*. To talk to *me*. To include *me*."

Rordan saw her, all right. He had seen her from the first moment he walked into Moorehall. "You have a right to that. Everyone does."

"Hmm," she said softly.

"I have no right to ask, but what is it you did that has your family keeping such a tight grip on you?"

Fianna gave him a guarded look before her gaze darted away.

"I shouldn't have asked," he said. "I'm sorry."

She pressed her lips together. "If I tell you, you'll look at me differently."

"I doubt that."

"You're the first person who has seen me, not my past. I don't want to ruin that."

He smiled at her to show he wasn't upset. "Fair enough."

"I should get back to the manor. Walk with me?"

"I'd like that."

They walked in comfortable silence. Rordan noticed that Fianna seemed more at ease than before, and he wondered if he had been a part of the transformation. He hoped so because she deserved it and more.

She walked just in front of him on the narrow path and glanced back often with a smile. The trail widened up ahead, which would allow them to walk together. He had come out to the lake to ensure he wouldn't be disturbed by anyone at the estate, but the evening couldn't have ended better if he had planned it.

Fianna smiled at him over her shoulder again when they both heard it. They halted, listening again. She started to divert from the path to see what it was, but Rordan grabbed her arm to stop her. He shook his head when she looked his way. Her frown told him that she was going to check it out regardless.

He moved up behind her and put his mouth to her ear. "It's two people who want some privacy."

She turned to face him and whispered, "I need to make sure they're our guests and not someone else."

"*I'm coming with you*," he mouthed.

She rolled her eyes, but there was a grin on her lips. They walked quietly through the woods, creeping closer to the couple. Rordan saw the firelight before he saw the pair. As soon as he did, his attention shifted to Fianna.

The moment she saw Dorcha and one of the male guards, her eyes widened in disbelief. However, it was the fury that surprised him. She opened her mouth to say something, but Rordan put his hand on her and jumped them to his cottage.

"Bastard!" she screamed.

Rordan released her and took a step back. "Because he was with another male?"

Fianna seemed too upset to speak. She paced back and forth, anger simmering from every pore. She needed to release that pent-up rage before she exploded, and Rordan knew just how to get her to do it.

He blocked her path. "Hit me."

"Get out of my way," she said through clenched teeth.

"Hit me," he told her again.

"I'm not going to hit you."

He swung at her, and just as he expected, she blocked him while delivering a blow to his midsection that had him staggering back. Rordan barely had time to raise his hands before she rushed him. They toppled the table and fell to the floor. He allowed her to do what she needed to do to get her anger out. When their tussle moved them through the door, and they rolled outside, he didn't stop her. He'd seen her train, had sparred with her, but sheer indignation ruled her now.

She straddled his hips, her fist aimed at his face, when she suddenly stopped, all the fight leaving her. Her face crumpled as she covered it with her hands. Rordan sat up and wrapped his arms around her as she cried.

Her arms wound around his neck, and she held him tightly. He imagined this was decades—if not centuries—of pent-up anger, resentment, and hurt that had finally broken free of their dam. Her body shook with her tears, gut-wrenching, soul-deep sobs that made him want to hunt down those who had wounded her and let them feel his fury.

They sat there for hours, long after her tears had dried. She was in his arms, and he had no desire to change that. Rordan couldn't remember the last time anything had felt so good, so...*right*.

"I was the bad seed," Fianna said, breaking the silence. "Just like my mother. My father told me demons had taken her. And me."

Rordan frowned at the term *demons* but let her speak.

"Da preached how clean and moral he and Dorcha were. How...proper. He told me that it was only because I was his blood that he would lower himself to help someone like me." She snorted. "I fought him at first. Told him there was nothing wrong with me. But if you're told often enough that you're dirty, that you're wrong, that your very existence is a blight, you begin to believe it. All those centuries, I believed him. Every word he spoke. Why would a father lie to their child? Even when he locked me in a small room, telling me it was the only way to drive out the demons, I trusted that he only had my best interests at heart."

Rordan tightened his arms around her while doing his best to hold in his anger, but he was losing the battle. And he feared he hadn't heard the worst of it yet.

"Even when I proved that the demons didn't rule me anymore, I wasn't trusted with anything. Da and Dorcha planned everything, decided every detail. And all the while, I was *happy* to be a part of it, glad that they had given me a second chance."

The indignation in her voice fanned the flames of Rordan's wrath.

"I settled into my role quite easily. I did everything that was asked of me without question. All because I wanted so desperately to please my father and remain a part of the family. I'm not sure how he did it, but he made it so I felt that I would crumble to nothing without them. That I would, quite literally, die. How does that happen to someone? How do they not realize what's going on?"

Rordan closed his eyes, holding onto her for himself as much as Fianna.

She drew in a ragged breath and sniffed. "Everything I've based my life on has been shattered. Yet, I see now that it was just an illusion. A fantasy my father created, and Dorcha went along with. To think that I believed Dorcha and I had gotten past our childhood differences. My brother has shown his true self these past few days, proving that even his civility has been a deception to keep me in line, so I don't embarrass the family."

Rordan's eyes opened when she sat up and loosened her arms. There were tear streaks down her face. Her perfect ponytail had come loose, inky strands falling around her shoulders. She'd had the rug pulled out from under her, and she had wobbled a bit, but there was no doubt about the strength within her. It shone in her silver eyes, in the set of her shoulders.

"You asked what had happened in my past to indebt me to my family."

He shook his head. "You don't need to tell me."

She put a finger over his lips and smiled briefly. "I want to."

But she didn't continue. Her gaze lowered to his mouth as she softly ran the tip of a finger along his bottom lip. Heat seared Rordan, shooting straight to his cock. The breeze coming from the ocean cooled his skin and ruffled her hair. He loosened his hold long enough to tuck a strand behind her ear.

"My mother left when I was very young. I have no memory of her, and we weren't allowed to speak of her. If she came up, Da flew into a rage. He didn't like me to have friends or to leave the house. He never shackled Dorcha as he did me. And when I came of age, I left. I told him I didn't need him or his rules." Fianna smiled softly before she swallowed. "I went to Dublin with some friends, and I began a life there. I lived like any other Fae. I toyed with one human once, but I found it distasteful, so I stayed away from them."

Rordan wiped away a fresh tear that rolled down her cheek, his heart breaking for her.

"The *demons* my father claimed I had, the same ones that had taken my mother, were those that liked sex."

He jerked back, confused. "We're Fae. We're sexual creatures."

"I know," she replied with a soft smile. "And yet, somehow, he brainwashed me into thinking it was something horrible. My father preached often and loud about how perfect he and Dorcha were. How they never tainted themselves with carrying out such acts."

"I hate to call him a liar, but how does he think you and your brother got here?"

She lifted her shoulders in a shrug. "When I saw Dorcha tonight, I lost it. Not because he was with a male but because he was having sex. Something my father claimed he wouldn't degrade himself to do. Dorcha was the standard, and I had to live up to that."

"You do understand that they're having sex. They've always had it."

"That realization slammed into me tonight." Her voice softened into a whisper as she gazed at him with longing. "There's nothing wrong with me. There's nothing wrong with sharing my body with someone. Especially someone that has filled my thoughts and dreams since I laid my eyes upon him."

Rordan slid his hands up her back as he moved his head closer. There was still time to pull away, still time to control his longing. He acknowledged the moment and let it go because there was no way he could walk away from Fianna.

He pressed his mouth to hers as she wound her arms around his neck again. Their lips brushed, once, twice. The next time, their tongues met, and all that mattered was the beautiful, amazing female in his arms.

CHAPTER FOURTEEN

The desire that rushed through her was intoxicating, Rordan's kiss exhilarating. His hands moved all over her, touching and caressing. She couldn't remember the last time she had felt this sexy, this desired.

This…*wanted.*

The night breeze rushed over their heated skin. She slid her fingers into his hair, and his lips traveled from her mouth down her neck. She dropped her head back, giving him better access. A shiver ran through her when he touched a pleasure point.

She gasped in delight when he fisted her hair and gently tugged her head back farther as he removed their clothes with magic. His other hand caressed her from her stomach up to her breasts. Her nipples puckered instantly as she felt the sea air against her skin. His mouth closed over a turgid peak and gently suckled, causing her to moan at the rush of pleasure.

He released her hair. She sat up, and they came together in a scorching kiss filled with raw need. Rordan gripped her hips and lifted her so that she hovered over his cock. She wanted to touch him, to feel him, to put him into her mouth, but her hunger was too great. And he knew it.

She tore her lips from his as he lowered her, his thick arousal slowly filling her body. Fianna looked at Rordan to find him gazing at her as if she were something special, and her heart skipped a beat. Their mouths came together once more as their bodies began to move. His hands were all over her body, touching and caressing. He knew just how to move, just how to hold her to give her the most pleasure.

Her hands were just as busy, running over his broad shoulders and the thick sinew of his arms and chest. She couldn't get enough of his body, his touch, his kisses. It might have been a long time since she had given in to her desires, but she still knew that there was something special happening between her and Rordan.

He moved faster, sending her tumbling toward an orgasm. It hit her suddenly, overtaking her and stealing her breath. The force of the release flung her into an abyss of ecstasy and bliss she never wanted to come back from. All she could do was cling to him as her body shattered into a thousand pieces before slowly coming back together again.

Rordan's eyes had darkened, the desire enveloping them. She moved her hips faster, wanting him to experience the same pleasure she had. His fingers dug into her hips as their bodies moved against each other until he shouted and climaxed. She held him tightly, just as he had held her earlier during what had felt like one of the darkest moments of her life.

They remained locked together until their breaths evened out. Then Rordan rolled them to the side. Fianna wasn't at all surprised to find a blanket beneath them. They shared a smile as he pulled out of her and gathered her in his arms as he settled onto his back. She released a long breath and stared at the landscape. She could just make out the darkened, rolling cliffs that fell away to the sea.

She had been so angry when Rordan brought her here that she hadn't noticed anything. Even after she'd finished crying and told her story, her memories had filled her mind. No other person in the universe knew her past the way Rordan now did. Getting the words out had left her feeling as if a huge weight had been lifted from her shoulders.

He kissed her forehead, causing her to smile. She became drowsy, her eyes heavy until she could no longer keep them open. She drifted off to sleep, slumbering peacefully. Dreams of Rordan woke her.

Her hands slid over his chest as she recalled not getting to have her fun with his body. She pushed up to look down at him. His eyes opened as his lips curved seductively. As she leaned down to kiss him, one of his hands came up to cup the back of her head.

How she loved his kisses. It would be so easy to lay there and kiss him until the end of time, but she wanted a chance to get a good look at him. Fianna ended the kiss and smoothed her hands over his chest and abdomen. She marveled at his chiseled abs and trim hips. She bent and placed her lips against his skin, kissing him lightly. Everywhere her hands went, her lips followed, licking and kissing.

Only when she had covered his entire torso did she look lower. His cock was hard, straining. She gently wrapped her fingers around it, remembering how good he had felt inside her. Fianna stroked his length, coming to learn the velvety skin with steel beneath. She glanced at his face to find him staring at her with hooded eyes, his hands fisted in the blanket.

She grinned, holding his gaze as she bent toward his arousal. His chest rose and fell rapidly, his lips parted. Then she parted *her* lips and wrapped them around his cock. Rordan moaned and whispered her name. She lavished attention on his arousal, bringing him to the brink of release. She wanted to push him over the edge, but he had other ideas.

Before she knew it, she was on her back with Rordan between

her legs. The first lash of his tongue on her sex made her eyes roll
back in her head. Desire tightened something low in her belly with
each flick of his tongue. When he pushed a finger inside her, she
teetered on the edge of climax.

Suddenly, Rordan rose over her and thrust inside. Fianna
wrapped her legs around him as he began to move faster, driving
deeper, harder. With each plunge, the pleasure intensified. Until she
peaked. The ecstasy was blinding, her body awash with the
astonishing, incredible sensations. But she didn't go alone. Rordan
joined her, sharing in the delightful bliss.

Within moments, Fianna was asleep.

Rordan woke her by kissing her shoulder. He was snuggled
behind her as she used his arm as a pillow. She rolled to face him,
knowing what he needed—because it was the same thing she
wanted.

They came together throughout the rest of the night, touching
and kissing as they made love, each time different from before. Once
they were spent, they would rest for a while, then start all over.
Sometimes, she was the one to wake him. Other times, he woke her.
But always they reached for each other. Always, they came together.

They lay wrapped in each other's arms when Fianna saw the
first streaks of dawn. She wasn't ready for the night to be over. The
light of day would bring the need for decisions she wasn't prepared
to make.

"Not yet," Rordan whispered as he scooped her into his arms
and jumped them inside the house to his bed.

He covered them as she rested her cheek on his chest and threw
her leg over his. He wrapped an arm around her and kissed her
forehead. She smiled as she fell into a deep, dreamless sleep—the
kind of rest she hadn't had in centuries.

A clap of thunder startled Fianna awake.

"Easy," Rordan said as he rubbed his hand up and down her
back.

"How long did I sleep?"

He put his other arm behind his head. "Several hours."

She should get back to the manor and Dorcha, but she didn't

want to leave. She didn't want any part of her family anymore. The blinders were off, and now that she saw what they had done to her—what she had allowed them to do—she wouldn't be party to any of it again.

"How are you doing?" Rordan asked.

Fianna shrugged and blew out a breath. "Physically, I feel great. Mentally and emotionally, I'm still struggling with everything that happened last night. With Dorcha," she added, just in case Rordan thought she meant him.

He played with the ends of her hair. "I don't know many who wouldn't feel as you do. What I can tell you is that there is nothing wrong with what we did last night. All night."

She chuckled, thinking of the many and various ways they had made love. "All night, indeed."

"Do you regret it?"

"Not a single moment."

"Good." He tightened his arm around her, briefly hugging her against him.

She drew in a deep breath. "I don't want to return to Moorehall."

"Then don't."

"Dorcha will look for me."

Rordan leaned away to look at her. "You don't answer to him. You answer only to yourself."

The intensity of his gaze made her grin. "I know."

"I hope you do. If you don't want to go back there or have any dealings with your family, you don't have to. No matter what anyone else says. And family will always attempt to guilt you into doing whatever they want."

"Is that what happened to you? Is that why you hate your family?"

Rordan looked away, a muscle jumping in his jaw. "There was only one good person in my family, and that was my mother."

"*Was?*"

"She died many years ago."

Fianna's heart hurt for him. "I'm so sorry, Rordan."

"I like to think things would've been different with her there, but I don't know how true that statement is."

"You remember her, though?"

His lips softened. "Aye. I remember her."

"There's a chance my mother is out there somewhere. I'd like to find her."

"Then do it. You've heard your father's side of the story. It's time you hear hers."

She happened to agree with him. "I'll do that. First, I'm going to tell Dorcha that he's on his own."

"Don't go back there."

Something in his tone, and the look in his eyes, made Fianna frown. She sat up and searched his face. "Why do I get the feeling you're saying that for more than just me talking to my brother?"

"Because things aren't as they seem with your brother or what he's doing."

Fianna's heart thudded painfully in her chest. "Why are you here? Why did you really come to the first meeting?"

"To see what your brother was about."

"No," she said with a shake of her head. "It's more than that. I know it."

Rordan sat up and raked his hands down his face. He sighed and then looked at her. "I would tell you if I could."

Her heart plummeted to her feet. "No."

"The last thing I ever expected was you."

"Who sent you?"

Rordan shook his head. "I can't tell you that."

"Are you here to assassinate Dorcha?"

"No."

She blew out a relieved breath. "And Ruarc? Is he with you?"

"He's not."

"Are you the people who have my father?"

Rordan shot her a hurt look. "No."

"But you know who does."

He shook his head and swung his legs over the side of the bed. "I told you that I couldn't give you answers."

"That is an answer. If you didn't, you would've told me."

Rordan twisted to look at her. "I'd love nothing more than to tell you everything."

"What I confessed last night should be enough to prove that I'm not with my family, despite what I told you before. Do you doubt me?"

Sincerity filled his gaze. "I don't. I know you spoke from the heart last night. If your father hadn't been taken, I'd hunt him down myself and show him what I think of what he's done to you."

Fianna scooted off the bed and saw, for the first time, the damage she had caused the previous night in her rage. She snapped her fingers, putting everything back the way it had been. Then she called her clothes to her.

"You're leaving," Rordan said.

She wrapped her arms around her middle, not sure what to do about anything. "I'm trying to figure out what to do. I've seen my family for who they really are, and now I learn that you aren't who I've believed you to be either. Is Rordan even your name?"

"Rordan Dovecoat," to be exact.

Her eyes widened as shock poured through her. Everyone knew the Dovecoat family. They were the wealthiest of all the Light.

And a family everyone wanted as their ally.

CHAPTER FIFTEEN

Rordan cringed at the recognition he saw in Fianna's eyes. "Now you know why I don't tell anyone."

"You're *that* Rordan?" she asked, amazement filling her face. "But...but I thought you had died."

He threw out his arms. "Obviously, I didn't."

"You should tell your family."

"I like things just the way they are."

She raked her fingers through her long locks, untangling the strands. "Is your family as dysfunctional as mine?"

"Everyone's family is dysfunctional. But to answer your

question, yes." Rordan then scooted back so he leaned against the headboard and patted the mattress.

Fianna didn't hesitate to crawl back onto the bed. She gathered some pillows at the foot and used them to lay her head on so she could look at him. Then she raised her brows.

He bit back a smile. "As you know, my family has influence. Their wealth has given them that. My two sisters were older, and while my father told them the eldest would inherit, he changed his mind after I was born, and named me heir."

"It's his right."

"Yes, it is, but that didn't matter to them. They were much older than me and had gotten used to having certain privileges. For a long time, I lived in a bubble, protected from harsh realities. My father wanted me to act a certain way, the *Dovecoat* way. I had other ideas. My mother was the one who kept the family together. She calmed frayed nerves and soothed ruffled feathers. But there was an entire world for me to see. I left as soon as I could, and it wasn't long before I found some friends. They weren't good Light. I quickly learned how to defend myself to stay alive. We got into some trouble, but when the authorities learned who I was, the charges were dropped."

"Yikes," Fianna said.

Rordan nodded as he laced his fingers behind his head. "Knowing that I could get away with just about anything sent me down a debauched path. I soon left those friends and found different ones, who were even worse. My fighting skills continued to improve, but I made one bad decision after another with no regard for anyone or anything. I was, for all intents and purposes, walking a fine line between Light and Dark. That went on for some time. Finally, I took a good, hard look at my life and realized that I wasn't the person I wanted to be. So, I went back home to sort out my life. Mum welcomed me, but my father and sisters had other ideas.

"They thought I had come for money, when all I needed was time to myself and away from my associates, who weren't too keen on me changing my ways. Mum convinced my father of that. Unfortunately, my sisters found my friends—and my enemies—and let them know where I was. My acquaintances were peeved that I had abandoned them, and my foes decided it was prime time to strike and remove me for good. It all happened my third night back."

Rordan dropped his arms as memories of that night engulfed him. The screams of his mother, the heat of the fire. "The house was heavily warded, but it wasn't enough. I was at the back of the estate in a small cottage because my father couldn't stand the sight of me. I saw the flames at the main house first. I ran to the manor and found my mother being assaulted. The culprits were fighting with the family security, as well. I immediately went after those attacking my mum. I didn't care what happened to me, only that she wasn't hurt. I don't remember much of the fight. When I came to, they were all dead. But…when I turned to my mother, she had already breathed her last. I didn't even get to her before she turned to ash. The only thing I wanted to do was kill those responsible. I joined the security team. A few who attacked were smart enough to get away, but most died that night.

"The fire was extinguished, but there was nothing I could do about my mother. I was kneeling beside her ashes when my father walked in. He took one look at what was left of Mum and ordered me out of the house—and his life. He banished me from the family. I didn't care. I had lost my mother, and I was grieving. They promptly forced me out of the house. I knew I wouldn't be allowed at Mum's memorial, and I wasn't, though for a different reason."

Fianna sat up and put her hand on his leg, sorrow in her beautiful silver eyes. "What happened?"

"My sisters were waiting for me when I left the estate. As soon as I saw them, I told them about Mum, but they didn't seem to care. In fact, they weren't shocked about the attack. They admitted to facilitating the entire event, though it wasn't supposed to be Mum who died, it was supposed to have been me. The words barely registered before I was assaulted and left for dead."

"No wonder you can't stand your family. But you should tell your father the truth."

Rordan twisted his lips. "It wouldn't do any good. He believes Mum would still be alive if I hadn't come home. And he's right."

"They are your family. You're supposed to be able to turn to them in times of need."

"Not mine," he replied.

Fianna studied him for a moment. "There's more to the story, isn't there?"

He frowned, trying to think what could've led her to that conclusion.

"You were left for dead, yet here you are, on another path than your previous one."

"People change."

She gave him a pointed look. "You've had that same expression on your face each time you said you couldn't tell me something. That look was there when you spoke of the attack."

Fek. She was good. Rordan met her gaze and shrugged.

"I wish you trusted me."

"I do," he told her. "But there are rules I must follow."

She gave him a sad smile. "Are these people you're with good?"

"They are. There might be some who would disagree."

"Like Dorcha?" she asked with a laugh.

Rordan took her hand and tugged her to him. "Don't go back to Moorehall. I'm begging you."

"Is something going to happen to my brother? Are you going to do something to him?"

"There is potential for something dire to happen, and you'd be wise to stay far away. None of it involves me. At this point."

She swallowed as she rested her head on his chest. "I might not particularly care for Dorcha, or even some of the other guests he invited, but I can't just stand by and allow them to be harmed. Tonight is our final meeting. This is when Dorcha picks who moves into the group."

Rordan stared at the far wall, his mind going over everything. The Fae Others were going to arrive tonight—the same night as the meeting. That couldn't be a coincidence. "What happens to those who aren't chosen?"

"What do you mean?"

"Are they angry? Do they come back and attend more meetings, hoping to be chosen?"

Fianna was quiet for a moment, then she sat up and looked at him. "I have no idea. It was never part of my job."

"You were at the other meetings. Do you not attend the final ones?"

"Well, in a way. Dorcha puts the people into two groups. They have no idea if they've been chosen or not. They each go into separate rooms. I follow Dorcha, and the servants show the others out."

Rordan rubbed his hand over his chin. "Dorcha riles everyone up in his early speeches. Everyone who comes back has similar views and wants to see them carried out. I can't imagine there haven't been some who were angry at not being chosen. I still have an issue about Dorcha picking people."

"It was how Da wanted it. I didn't question things then. And if I did, I was told it wasn't my concern. But you're right. There should have been some scuffles or at least raised voices. I can't remember a single instance. No guards said anything. No servants either. That's not right. Now that I'm looking at everything in a new light, I have to ask myself why others wouldn't see that Dorcha is selective."

"They know," Rordan told her. "That's what makes him so appealing to the Fae elite."

Her brows drew together. "Don't they realize that if the Fae are united under one council, there won't be any more nobility?"

"They won't give that up easily. But they don't care. They think they can have a council and still retain their ranking in society if they're part of the movement."

She sighed wearily as she looked away. "I can't believe I was so blind to all of this."

"Your eyes are open now."

Her gaze slid back to him. "Let me help you."

"What?" he asked, taken aback by her words.

"Let me help you with whatever you're doing. I don't want to be a part of what my family is doing. Because the more I learn, the more I question everything. I thought we were doing something good to change our culture. I've done what they've told me to all these years, and I can't be a part of something that is ultimately a lie."

Rordan brought her hand to his lips as he kissed it. There was no way he would let her anywhere near Moorehall, especially tonight. Fianna was special, and he would do whatever it took to keep her safe—even if she hated him for it. So, he lied. "If you can help, I'll let you."

"Thank you. I need to do this." She curled up against him.

He closed his eyes, hating the lie. "I know."

"I wish you weren't going back to the manor."

"I don't have a choice."

"Dorcha will ask if you've seen me," she said.

Rordan imagined punching Dorcha in the face. "I suspect he will."

"What are you going to tell him?"

"What do you want me to tell him?"

She was silent for a moment, then she raised her head and smiled at him. "Tell him the truth."

Rordan chuckled. He could well imagine Dorcha's response. "Are you sure that's wise?"

"I don't know," she said in a soft voice. "A part of me is worried about my father. Despite what he's done, he's still my da. Do you think he's being treated fairly by those who have him?"

"I honestly can't say."

"I'm angry at both of them, but I don't want them to die."

Rordan kissed the top of her head, unsure how to respond.

"Your silence makes me worry that it's a possibility."

He squeezed his eyes closed, debating with himself whether he should tell her anything about the Others. The group was dangerous, and the Fae needed to know about them. He couldn't tell her about the Reapers, but he could make a valid argument for sharing the information about the Fae group.

Rordan moved her to look in her eyes. "Pay close attention to what I'm about to tell you. It's important."

She nodded in response.

"When Usaeil was still alive, did you ever hear anything about a group called the Others?"

Fianna's brows drew together as she considered that for a moment. "I think I heard it in passing. Oh, wait! I heard Dorcha say something about them. He seemed very impressed."

"Too few understand who the Others actually were. They were a group of six. A Light and Dark Fae, a *mie* and *drough* Druid from this realm, as well as a pair from another realm. They combined their magic to battle the Dragon Kings."

She jerked her head back. "You can't be serious."

"I am. Usaeil was the Dark Fae. The mortals on Earth were brought here by the Druids from the other realm because of the magic. They wanted it and intended to rid this planet of the Dragon Kings. It backfired on them, however, and they were defeated. Or so we thought until a few months ago."

Unease filled Fianna's eyes. "Why do you say that?"

"We ran into a group of Fae who displayed the same characteristics as the Others. Light and Dark, working together. Some Druids also want their own group."

"Light and Dark Fae don't work well together," Fianna said. "That's why the council isn't coming together easily. I don't know many Druids, but I know that *mies* and *droughs* don't get along either."

Rordan shot her a wry smile. "Exactly. Yet they are joining forces and combining their magic to become something altogether stronger."

"Are you saying that's who has my father?"

"I am."

She got off the bed and began to pace. He could see her mind working through everything.

"I told you all of that so you'd be on the lookout," Rordan said.

She halted and looked at him. "These Fae Others are coming to Moorehall."

"They are."

"I have to go. There are innocents there. My guards. The servants. The guests."

Rordan rose from the bed and walked to her, taking her hands. "I'll start getting everyone out that I can, but I can't do anything if I'm worried about you. I need you to remain behind. Please. I will make sure the innocent aren't harmed."

She searched his face for long moments, then nodded. "I'm trusting you."

"I won't let you down. I promise."

When she nodded, he pulled her against him and wrapped his arms around her. The very thought of her hurt—or worse—left him with a cold feeling inside. That's how he knew that he had fallen in love with Fianna sometime during the night.

CHAPTER SIXTEEN

Somewhere in the wilds of Ireland…

He could feel it as surely as he could feel the rain falling upon his face. Evil was out there, a living, breathing entity that had to be stopped.

Xaneth grabbed his head with his hands as the pain within began pounding violently. The sound pierced his skull, deafening him and causing his stomach to roil viciously. He dropped to his knees onto the wet grass and pitched forward. His hands flattened against the ground, just barely stopping his face from slamming into it.

He gagged from the pain, his stomach heaving again and again, though there was nothing to expel. Finally, the retching halted, and he fell onto his side. He was soaked with sweat, and the cool breeze and rain cooled his skin as the last vestiges of the headache subsided. His eyes closed, and even though he tried not to sleep, he was pulled under.

At first, he drifted easily in the darkness while his body recuperated. Xaneth let himself relax and lowered his guard. The moment he did, the nightmare reared to life. The monster Usaeil had created in his mind returned. Xaneth came awake the instant he heard the roar. He lay there, breathing heavily as he discerned if he was still dreaming or not.

The cry of a falcon above allowed the tension to ease from his body. There had been no birds in the living nightmare. He rolled onto his back to continue watching the bird. His clothes were damp, telling him that the rain had halted some time ago. But he didn't care. The hillside was peaceful, the bird graceful as it soared above him. For just a heartbeat, Xaneth could forget the past. Disregard the driving need to stamp out all malevolence on the realm.

A child's shrill laughter punctured the peace. Xaneth pushed to his feet and began heading downhill, away from the child. He couldn't shake that he needed to find someone, that it was vitally important. But the need to stamp out the wicked was too pervasive.

Xaneth turned toward the feel of the evil. And with one thought, teleported.

CHAPTER SEVENTEEN

Fianna paced the cottage. She was anxious about Rordan facing her brother alone, but more than that, she couldn't wrap her head around the news of the Others. Or the fact that her brother could very well be involved with them.

And she by extension.

She halted and closed her eyes as she searched her mind, trying to remember the conversations she'd overheard between her father and Dorcha. They spoke a lot about destiny, about their family being a part of something important. Still, no matter how hard she searched her memories, she couldn't remember hearing anything about the Others.

Then again, her father and brother had been very careful about what they said in front of her. They never spoke freely when she was around. All that time, Fianna had believed it was her fault for losing their trust. How many times had her father said that to her? Too many to count. Now that she knew the truth, she couldn't stop the anger that simmered like lava bubbling within a volcano before an eruption.

Her family had lied to her, brainwashed her, and made her believe the most horrible things about her mother. She'd thought for a moment that she could sort through the lies and deceptions. Then she realized that everything her father and brother had told her had been nothing but falsehoods and fabrications.

She had bowed and scraped, doing everything she could think of to be forgiven. Only to discover that she had nothing to be sorry for.

They had stripped her of who she was, while attempting to remake her into what they wanted. And they had nearly succeeded. Fianna snorted. *Nearly*? No, they had succeeded. If Rordan hadn't come into her life, she would still be on that path, begging for any bits of praise from her father or inclusion by her brother. Her life, in fact, had been nothing but a lie.

She thought about looking for her mother, but her thoughts swung back to Rordan. It didn't sit well with her that he couldn't tell her specifics about the group he was with. If she didn't trust him, she wouldn't have revealed her past to him or agreed to wait while he dealt with Dorcha and the Fae Others.

But he was alone. Rordan was an exceptional warrior, but he would still be outnumbered. Unless he had the element of surprise. It was the route she would take. As hard as it was, Fianna decided to wait at the cottage as she had promised.

Eoghan stared out over the rolling green hills of western Ireland. The trail he and his Reapers had followed for Xaneth had led them to this place. It was quiet and peaceful, and if he listened closely, he could hear the sound of the waves crashing against the cliffs. He could see white cottages dotting the landscape in the distance.

"He was here," Aisling stated.

Eoghan's gaze swung to find her squatting next to a patch of grass that was still trampled as if someone had been lying on it.

Aisling lifted her gaze to Eoghan. "Though it looks like he was here for some time, he's still ahead of us."

"It's taking too long for us to track him," Torin said, agitation in his voice.

Eoghan turned his head to the newest Reaper. Balladyn wasn't part of his team, but the former King of the Dark and legendary Light warrior was with them looking for Xaneth. Balladyn faced away from them, his long, black and silver hair falling down his back as he looked out to the sea.

Eoghan glanced at the others to see them gathered together. Then he walked to stand beside Balladyn. "What is it you see?"

"Did you ever think it might be better if we left Xaneth alone?" Balladyn asked.

Eoghan crossed his arms over his chest. "Aye. But it doesn't matter what I think. Death gave us an order. We must follow it."

"We have no idea what horrors Usaeil made Xaneth suffer. He won't be the same."

"No doubt, you're right."

Balladyn's head turned, his red eyes locking with Eoghan's before glancing behind him at the others. "Do the rest understand that we might not have a choice about what we do with Xaneth once we find him?"

Eoghan knew that Balladyn's words were directed at Aisling. The female Reaper was intent on locating Xaneth far more than even Death herself. It was something Eoghan hadn't wanted to look at too closely, but he knew there might come a time when he had no other choice.

"You aren't the only one who thought of Xaneth as a friend," Eoghan said. "He left his mark on many."

Balladyn's gaze moved to the distance once more. "Sometimes, it's better to end the monster a Fae has become, rather than attempt to redeem them."

"You were redeemed."

"Exactly," he said, disgust dripping from his tone. "I should've been put down the moment I turned Dark."

Eoghan dropped his arms to his sides and faced the Fae. "No one in that position would've been able to withstand the darkness. You shouldn't carry that."

"Rhi withstood it."

"Rhi was in there for weeks. You were locked in the dungeon and tortured for *decades*. It isn't the same. And even Rhi succumbed. She admits that to this day."

Balladyn looked at the ground. "This isn't about me. This is about Xaneth." He looked at Eoghan. "I've watched you each time we've tracked Xaneth. You know, just as I do, that Usaeil might have turned a good Fae into a monster. She tormented him for a long time. He hasn't harmed anyone yet, but he might."

"I do know. Let's keep it to ourselves for the moment."

Balladyn looked over his shoulder once more. "You have a great group of warriors. The best I've seen."

"It's why Death chose each of us. And you."

"Hmmm. But I don't fit in anywhere."

"If there's one thing I've learned about being a Reaper, it's that Death always has a plan."

Balladyn looked at Eoghan and bowed his head. "I will do my best to remember that."

"Eoghan," Cathal said as he walked up. "We have no idea which direction Xaneth went. For all we know, he teleported to the other side of the world. We've fanned out and tried to get a direction as we have in the past, but we're coming up empty."

"He's stayed in Ireland up until now," Balladyn pointed out.

Eoghan considered that and nodded. "He's gone nowhere near the Light Castle or the Dark Palace. In fact, he's gone to places much like this one—remote and quiet."

"Then why leave?" Cathal asked.

Balladyn faced them. "Because his mind is in complete and utter turmoil. These places are serene, but it isn't enough."

"What is making him leave, then?" Aisling asked as she walked to them, flinging one of the many small braids of her hair over her shoulder.

Torin, Bradach, and Dubhan made their way over.

"We won't know that until we catch up with him," Balladyn told the group.

Torin looked at Eoghan, a frown forming. "Does anyone else realize how close we are to Rordan?"

"Shite," Aisling murmured.

Eoghan slid his gaze to Balladyn before turning his head and looking in the direction of Achill Island, which was also the direction Balladyn had been staring. Eoghan jerked his attention to Balladyn. "Did you know?"

"I wasn't positive, but it was a consideration," the former King of the Dark answered.

Bradach flattened his lips. "Bloody hell. This can't be good."

"When is it ever?" Dubhan asked sarcastically.

Eoghan drew in a deep breath and released it. "Rordan would have alerted us if Xaneth was there. Until he does, we find other areas where Xaneth might have gone."

As he spoke, he let his gaze linger on each Reaper, stopping on Aisling. She was normally at ease under pressure, but she was restless and anxious. It had started the moment they found Usaeil's home and discovered that Xaneth had been held there. Eoghan thought about asking her if there was more to things, but he wouldn't have appreciated Cael doing that to him. So, Eoghan kept his thoughts to himself. For the time being. But he would keep a close watch on Aisling.

Everyone moved away, using their magic to search the ground and air, trying to discern where Xaneth was or had gone. Everyone, that is, except for Torin.

"What is it?" Eoghan asked.

"I've got a bad feeling."

"We'll find Xaneth."

Torin shook his head of black hair when Eoghan spoke. "About

Rordan."

"He knows to call for us if he needs help."

"The last time I had this feeling, Usaeil murdered Balladyn."

Eoghan's brows snapped together as he stared at Torin. "I never heard you say anything that day."

"Because I didn't. I kept it to myself because I wasn't sure if it was about Balladyn or someone else."

"Do you normally have these kinds of…feelings?"

Torin issued a quick shake of his head. "This is the second time. It might be nothing. I could be hyperaware because we're looking for Xaneth."

"And we both know that Rordan is dealing with the Fae Others," Eoghan finished. He ran a hand over his mouth. "Fek."

"I could go. Stay veiled and keep an eye on things. Rordan shouldn't be alone against the Others."

"I agree, but it wasn't my call." Eoghan sighed loudly. "The only way Rordan is able to complete his mission is if he's there alone. He's navigating a minefield."

"Which is why someone should be there to watch his back."

Eoghan might think otherwise, but he would obey Death. "We know from Dubhan that the Fae Others like to make sure there isn't anyone veiled around them. If they find you, Rordan could lose whatever ground he's managed to gain."

A muscle ticked in Torin's jaw. "I know Rordan can take care of himself. It's just…well…"

"We're a family," Eoghan finished for him. "I know. I understand how you feel. There used to be only seven Reapers. Now there are fifteen."

They both looked at Balladyn. There were only seven Reapers in each team. Eoghan had asked Death what she planned to do with Balladyn, but she hadn't answered him. That could mean she wasn't ready to divulge her plans. Or that she didn't know.

"Rordan will be fine," Torin said and walked away.

Eoghan wasn't sure if Torin said it to convince himself or Eoghan. With one last look toward the west, Eoghan began searching for clues to find Xaneth.

CHAPTER EIGHTEEN

The promise Rordan had made Fianna was forefront in his mind when he returned to Moorehall. There was still no sign of Ruarc, which concerned him. Everything around the manor appeared as it had when he and Fianna had departed.

Rordan casually walked through the house, nodding at those he passed. He turned a corner to head out a back entrance to the forest for another look around for Ruarc, when someone stepped in his way. He drew up short and found none other than Dorcha.

"Where is she?" the Fae demanded.

"Who?"

"Don't play the idiot. You know of who I speak."

Rordan clasped his hands behind his back as he noted Dorcha's sweaty brow and the tightness around his mouth. Fianna wanted Rordan to tell her brother the truth, but Rordan knew that was a bad idea. "Perhaps if you told me a name."

"My sister," Dorcha said between clenched teeth, spittle flying from his mouth.

Rordan looked down at his shirt and calmly wiped away the droplets of spit. Only then did he raise his gaze to Dorcha. "Why would you think I know anything about your sister?"

"Because you were gone last night."

"And how would you know that?"

Dorcha's nostrils flared in fury. "Where's Fianna."

"I have no idea."

"You're lying."

Rordan shrugged, his lips twisting. "Believe what you wish." He started to move around Dorcha when the Fae blocked him.

"I could have you killed."

Rordan glared at Dorcha. He would like nothing more than for Dorcha to attack so Rordan could punch him in the face. But that wasn't going to happen. Dorcha wasn't a fighter. He had people who did his dirty work for him.

He took a step closer to Dorcha and lowered his voice. "Give it your best shot."

"Wanker," Dorcha mumbled beneath his breath as he walked around Rordan.

Rordan watched Dorcha's departing back until he was out of sight. Only then did Rordan go outside. He leisurely strolled the area, but he was on full alert. Rordan took note of where the guards were and if anyone looked out of place. It was a testament to Fianna's management that the guards didn't miss a beat in her absence. They knew exactly what to do. Unfortunately, none of them stood a chance against the Others.

The hours dragged on. Rordan kept his gaze on the passage of the sun. The Fae had told Dorcha they would return that night, and Rordan took that literally. One look confirmed that as Dorcha grew increasingly more agitated with each passing minute.

Rordan had no wish to attend the final meeting that evening, but he didn't have much of a choice. He changed into evening attire as was requested and gave himself a few moments alone in his chamber. He wasn't afraid of the Others, but he wasn't a fool either. The organization needed to be stopped before they got more of a foothold, and in order to do that, he needed the rest of the Reapers. The instant he saw the Others, he would call out to Eoghan so the Reapers could take them on.

Rordan's walk around the estate hadn't been just to pass the time. He had scouted locations where he thought the Others might attack. A couple of sites were prime for just such an event. They were close to the manor but gave whoever held the position an advantage. No doubt the Others had already surveyed those locales, as well.

He smiled and imagined their faces as the Reapers surrounded them. It would all have to be done delicately, though. No one at the manor could know of the Reapers' existence. It wouldn't be the first time the Reapers had fought in front of Fae.

Rordan slowly released a breath as the last light of the sun disappeared behind the mountains. He adjusted the sleeves of his shirt beneath his jacket and turned on his heel to exit his room. As he walked down the corridor, he heard yelling coming from Dorcha's chamber as the Fae shouted at someone about finding Fianna. Rordan hoped that she kept her promise and remained at the cottage. Once this business with Dorcha and the Others was dealt with, he would get permission from Death to tell Fianna who he really was.

He knew Fianna held some affection for him. He wasn't sure how much, but he was willing to wait. He'd gone his entire life up to that point without her. Knowing that he had found her made it easier to wait—however long was needed for her to decide if she wanted him. The problem was that he wasn't sure Erith would authorize it if there was a chance that Fianna might not choose him. The secrecy of the Reapers was paramount.

That secret and a Reaper falling in love had nearly destroyed the first group. It had fractured them, with one Reaper killing others until Death stepped in. Bran had been banished to another realm but had managed to find his way back. And when he did, he'd made it his mission to annihilate the Reapers—and even Erith herself.

Bran had almost succeeded, but he hadn't counted on Death's and Cael's love for each other. That entire tragedy had opened Erith's eyes to what her Reapers needed. She relaxed the no-mates rule, but it was still a delicate situation. Because at the end of the day, no one could know about the Reapers.

Rordan ran his hand down his face as he reached the bottom of the stairs. The din of conversation pulled him to the dining room. As he stepped inside, he thought back to just a few nights earlier when he had seen Fianna out of her uniform. How he wished she were with him now.

He strode to the liquor station and ordered a whisky. As he took a drink, he surveyed the room. There were many similarities between the Fae and the mortals of the planet. There were many more differences, however. Some humans might think the Fae mimicked them with their social classes, servants, and such. But the truth was that the Fae had had all of that eons before the mortals ever came to this realm. That parallel was what made it easy for the Fae to fit in with the humans.

Rordan wished the other Reapers were there. Not because he wasn't capable of handling a fight, but because he couldn't stand the pomp and circumstance flouted so abundantly during dinners like this. It reminded him too much of his childhood and everything that he had run from.

His thoughts halted when Dorcha sauntered into the room. He didn't wear his easy smile from the earlier meetings. This time, it was forced, cold—just as his eyes were. Rordan had a feeling this was the real Dorcha. The other was merely an act, something that got him what he and his father wanted.

In a blink, Dorcha had his mask properly in place as he greeted his overeager guests. There were more people than before. Rordan recognized a few who had stayed overnight, but there were another twenty he didn't know. He turned to make his way to a quiet corner to observe the room when his eyes met ones he hadn't seen in years.

His stomach dropped to his feet as he stared into the face of his father.

"Rordan? Is that really you?"

He heard the disbelief in his da's voice, even as he tried to think of something to say, some lie to give.

Renault walked to him as he looked Rordan over. "Son. I-I thought you were dead."

Rordan noticed how his father had aged. Despite the lines upon his face, Renault still appeared as regal as ever. Rordan kept his voice low as he said, "You need to leave this place. Immediately."

"I won't. Not now that I've seen you. Look, son, I know some harsh things were said—"

Rordan wrapped a hand around his father's arm to lead him out and then leaned in close to whisper, "Now isn't the time for such talk. You need to leave *right now*. This has nothing to do with us or the past."

"Renault!"

Rordan briefly closed his eyes when he heard Dorcha call out his father's name. The time for his father's escape might very well have passed.

"Well, well, well," Dorcha said as he stopped before them. He looked from Rordan to Renault. "I see the resemblance now. Rordan, why didn't you tell me you were a Dovecoat?"

Rordan dropped his hand from his father's arm and faced Dorcha. "Personal preference."

Dorcha stared at him, a smirk forming. "It seems there is a lot about you I didn't know."

"I could say the same."

Dorcha's confidence faltered as his brows snapped together. "What's that supposed to mean?"

"I'm just wondering what everyone would think if they knew who you really were."

"They know who I am."

It was Rordan's turn to grin. "Do they? So, they know your surname as I do?"

The tension in the room ramped up. Rordan could see his father

S OBSESSION 127

looking between him and Dorcha. Thankfully, his father kept his mouth shut. Those around them had taken note that something was amiss. More and more of Dorcha's guests turned their attention to the three of them.

Rordan kept his expression impassive, though he was anything but. The jolt he'd felt at discovering his father had sent him for a loop. That, on top of his anger at Dorcha, had Rordan tied in knots. He was a warrior, a Fae of action. He wanted to attack, to do *something*. Remaining still and keeping quiet were the most difficult things he had done.

Finally, Dorcha bowed his head, giving the moment to Rordan. But that's all it would be. Rordan suspected the instant he tried to get his father out, they would be stopped. This was one issue Rordan had never thought to have.

"I'll leave," Renault whispered.

Rordan shook his head as he faced his father. "That ship has sailed."

"What do you need me to do?"

Rordan was taken aback by the fact that his father would ask him that. He studied his da's face, searched his eyes, but found nothing disparaging. "Stick with me and do everything I say."

"I can do that." Renault took a drink of wine as he looked over the rim of the glass to the other guests. "Can you tell me what's going on?"

"Not really. It isn't good, though."

"I pieced that together fairly quickly." There was a beat of silence. "You look good, son. I'd like to make up for the past, if you'll allow me."

Rordan turned his head away. At one time, he would've given anything to hear those words. But now? He wasn't the same person he had once been. Being betrayed by one's sisters and getting killed tended to change someone drastically.

"I'll do anything," Renault said.

Rordan swung his gaze back to his father. "There are somethings that can't be fixed."

"I was a fool. I turned into my father, the very thing I swore I would never do. When your mother was killed, I lashed out. It was inexcusable. When I finally came to my senses days later, your sisters told me you had died."

"Did they tell you how?"

Renault's black brows furrowed as he blinked in confusion. "They said you were attacked."

"Hmm."

"Obviously, your sisters were wrong."

Rordan didn't reply. He could've lied, but he chose to remain silent instead.

"I see you hold many secrets," Renault murmured.

Rordan glanced at the floor and shrugged. "Doesn't everyone?"

His father started to answer, but Dorcha interrupted as he called for everyone's attention. Rordan remained at the back of the room while everyone else moved forward to see Dorcha better. Renault stayed with him. Dorcha climbed up onto the stage, his gaze meeting Rordan's. There was a confrontation coming. Rordan had been looking forward to it, but now that his father was there, it could complicate things. At least, Fianna was safely away.

"Tonight is cause for celebration," Dorcha said with a smile.

The occupants of the room cheered, but Rordan knew it would be anything but.

CHAPTER NINETEEN

The location of the cottage was spectacular. Fianna stood outside on the cliffs and watched the majesty and mayhem of the sea. She'd spent the entire day with just her thoughts.

And there was much she needed to think about.

She had walked along the cliffs, basking in the sea air. No roads or other dwellings were near, which afforded her all the privacy she wanted. She had been surprised that the cottage had no wards. Setting them was something a Fae did the moment they stepped into a location they spent time in. But not Rordan.

That in and of itself confused her because she knew him to be an intelligent warrior. He studied people and places. He contemplated his attacks instead of being hasty. So why not put up wards? She didn't linger on that for long. The beauty of the place pulled her away from such worries and forced her thoughts inward.

Fianna couldn't remember the last time she'd had so much time to herself. It really did feel as if she had thrown off the shackles. She felt almost as light as a feather. But in the same instance, she was weighed down by the past and her part in it.

One by one, she went through her questions and tugged on the connecting threads. She delved deeply into memories she had forgotten. She looked at her life before her father had stepped in. And…she let herself drudge up every memory she had of her mother.

By the time Fianna finished, she was mentally and emotionally shattered. She lay back on the grass and watched the sky turn from pale blue to gray to black. Her internal struggles had resulted in her accepting the past because she couldn't change it. They had also helped her come to decisions regarding the present—and the future.

There was so much she wanted to tell Rordan. He had only been in her life for a short time, but he had made a huge impact. One thing was for certain—she had developed feelings for him. Strong ones. Feelings that were, in fact, love.

She smiled, thinking about it. But the grin quickly faded as her mind called up why Rordan was currently away. She blinked up at the stars. Different scenarios ran through her head. Some, where Rordan won. Others where her brother did.

Fianna sat up as a knot of unease filled her stomach.

From the moment Dorcha opened his mouth, nearly everyone in the room was enthralled. Sadly, Rordan might have been as well if he weren't aware of Dorcha's involvement with the Others.

"We could sneak out now," Renault whispered.

Rordan glanced at his father. "I have a feeling we won't be able to teleport out. Besides, I'm not going anywhere."

"I was afraid you would say that. How bad is it going to get?"

Rordan met his father's gaze. "Bad."

"I was never much of a warrior. My father had other plans for me. The same ones I had for you. But I'll do my part."

Rordan wanted to take his da up on the offer, but he didn't know the male standing before him. He never had. For all he knew, Renault could be in deep with the Others.

Renault's lips twisted ruefully. "You don't think you can trust me. I've not given you reason to think otherwise."

"I don't know you."

"Aye. If it helps, this is my third meeting. A friend told me about Dorcha, and I go to meetings when I'm able. I hear it's an honor to be asked to the final one."

Rordan looked at Dorcha on the stage, talking up his plans with those in the room nodding in agreement. They were lambs being led to slaughter.

"You don't have to tell me anything. Just let me help," Renault urged.

Rordan blew out a breath and nodded. He kept his voice low. "There will come a time those here are divided into two groups."

"Those who are chosen for the organization, and those who aren't," Renault confirmed with a nod. "I'm aware."

Rordan finished his whisky and set the glass on a nearby table, his gaze locked on Dorcha. "Be prepared. One group is accepted, but the other, I believe, won't be freed. I think they're taken somewhere to be held or killed."

"You can't be serious."

The surprise in his father's voice caused Rordan to send him a glance. "Oh, I am. Regardless of what group you're in, you need to get everyone away from the manor."

"And what are you going to do?"

"I'm going to end this tonight."

"Alone?" Renault asked in a tight voice. "That's suicide. Have you seen the guards? And I heard that Dorcha's sister is a phenomenal warrior."

An image of Fianna smiling up at him before they kissed flashed in his mind. "She is."

"Ah."

He shot his father a dark look. "What does that mean?"

"It's easy to see you're enamored with her."

Rordan didn't say otherwise. He sized up the room, noting the sentries placed in visible locations, and those that were hidden. He shifted his shoulders, hating the tightness of the jacket.

Suddenly, a door opened, and three males walked in. The lead Light from the Others, and two more. In between the two Fae was an older version of Dorcha. When Dorcha's eyes landed on the trio, his words halted. The confidence he'd exuded during his talk faded as dread filled his eyes. Wariness swept through the room.

"By the stars," Renault said. "That's Fearghal. I've not seen him in ages. At least not since he disappeared with his children. Bloody hell. Dorcha is his son."

Rordan clenched his teeth together as he stared at the Others. "Did you know who Dorcha was?"

"No. He was only called Dorcha. No surname attached. And, sadly, I never paid attention to the names of Fearghal's children. Rordan, that family is—"

"I'm aware. I'm also cognizant of the fact that not everyone is like their parents."

Dorcha cleared his throat and issued a shaky smile to the room. "Ladies and gentlemen, as I was saying, the night is drawing to a close. Each of you has shown your dedication and exuberance to the future of the Fae. While I'd love to take every one of you with me, unfortunately, that just isn't possible. You will be—"

"Why not?" Rordan interrupted. "Why can't everyone who agrees with your vision of the future be included? Why do you pick and choose? Why do you make everyone attend meeting after meeting?"

A female near Rordan nodded in agreement. "He has a point. I've already given a lot of money, and I was assured I'd be included in the organization."

"I was promised a spot, too," someone else said.

One by one, those in the crowd spoke of Dorcha's promise.

Dorcha raised his hands to quiet the room, but no one paid him any attention. His nervousness made the situation worse.

"This movement would gain much more ground if everyone who believed in it could join," a female in the front stated.

Dorcha issued a tense laugh before shooting a venomous look at Rordan. "I can assure everyone that you will each be a part of the organization."

Rordan's amusement of the situation vanished when the Dark got up on stage next to Dorcha and said something. Dorcha visibly paled and jerked his chin in Rordan's direction. The Others' Light leader turned his head and looked at Rordan with an icy smile. In the next instant, the Others led Fearghal out. The Fae whispered something else to Dorcha before following his group out.

"Get ready," Rordan told his father.

Dorcha swallowed and glanced at the exit. "We're going to be split into two groups to make things easier. When I call your name, I need you to move to the left side of the room."

But no one was listening to Dorcha anymore. They were talking amongst themselves, getting angrier by the moment. The guards looked around for any signs of Fianna, and the fact that she was nowhere to be found started to sink in.

Dorcha waved a guard to him. Rordan recognized him as Dorcha's lover. The two spoke in hushed tones before Dorcha once again tried to get the room's attention. Several people attempted to teleport out, only to discover that they couldn't.

"What's going on here?" someone demanded.

"Why can't we leave?"

"He's stopping us. Get him!"

While the guards protected him, Dorcha ran out the same door Fearghal and the Others had left through.

Rordan looked at his father. "Get those you can and make your way to an exit. Get out of the manor. Don't trust anyone but me. When you can, teleport out."

"When can I see you again?"

"We'll talk later," Rordan told him as he went after Dorcha and the Others.

He had to physically move some people out of his way. He pulled one male by the back of his jacket and shook him. "Dorcha's gone. Get out, now."

That was enough to get most in the room moving toward Renault, who waved people to him. Rordan then turned to the guards. It was their duty to protect Dorcha. Some of them he remembered from sparring. Some had even gone up against him and knew his skill. Rordan didn't want to hurt any of them, but he would. He needed to find the Others so he could call the Reapers and end everything.

"Let me pass," he told them.

The guard, Ella, nudged Leo. The two of them stepped aside and let Rordan through.

"You all should leave while you can." Rordan gave them a nod before running out the door.

But Dorcha had a head start. The house was a maze, and Dorcha could have gone in any number of directions.

"Fek," Rordan ground out. He came to a halt and looked one way and then the other before he smiled. "Of course," he murmured and rushed outside.

CHAPTER TWENTY

The grand manor stood like a sentry in the forest. Xaneth didn't see the beautiful architecture or the glittering decorations within. The stench of evil, the reek of iniquity was too overpowering.

He stared at the front door for long moments. Someone was speaking within, though he couldn't care less what was being said. He wasn't there to be entertained. He had come to remove the malevolent entity.

Xaneth walked around to the right of the manor, past the landscaping, and into a garden. Lights filtered through the window and spilled onto the shadowed ground. He glanced into the structure as he passed and saw a roomful of people, all looking in one direction. Suddenly, Xaneth halted. Someone in the room caught his attention.

He scanned the profiles yet didn't recognize anyone. But something had made him stop. He shook his head to loosen the thought that had prompted him to halt. Xaneth looked forward and drew in a deep breath. Then he continued on and made his way around a tall hedge when a figure stepped into his path.

One look at the female told Xaneth that she was a guard intent on preventing him from going forward. And that simply couldn't happen. He rushed her as she opened her mouth to speak. He lobbed a volley of magic into her chest, then slammed his hand into the same location, knocking her back to the ground. Xaneth remained on one knee, listening for others who might have heard the commotion. When he caught the sound of multiple sets of feet coming his way, he stood and gathered his magic and let the hedges hide him.

His magic built, growing stronger with each second. By the time the three guards found him, he lunged forward, throwing his hands up and out to release the magic. It crashed into the guards, knocking them flat on their backs.

Xaneth straightened and stepped over the fallen Fae as he continued his search for the evil. He weaved through the garden. He saw a figure rush off from the back of the house. Just as the sound of the occupants' voices spilled into the night and caught his attention. He looked toward the manor and the hurried, anxious Fae who fled the structure. He narrowed his gaze on them, but the evil that brought him there wasn't with them. The group attempted to teleport repeatedly, only to be stopped each time.

He glanced above him, wondering what spells were in place to keep him here. Not that it mattered. He wasn't going anywhere until he had finished what he came to do.

The group's voices drew his attention once more. An older Fae guided the others farther away from the manor. Finally, they reached a safe spot, and the others jumped to safety—all but the one who had aided them. To his surprise, Xaneth observed the older Fae rushing back into the manor, searching for something. Or someone.

When the Fae disappeared into the house, Xaneth swung his attention to the lone person he saw running into the night. They had gone in the direction of the evil. Perhaps they were one and the same. With a few whispered words of magic, ensuring a field no one could penetrate, he started walking again.

He was so fekked.

Dorcha slid to a halt, his head swinging from one direction to another. He needed to get far away from Moorehall. But every time he tried to teleport, something stopped him. Anger and fear ripped through him as sweat dripped from his forehead into his eyes.

He swiped at his brow, his mind racing, trying to find a way to save his own skin. He had been an idiot to think that the Others would keep up their side of the bargain and let him live once he had pointed out Rordan as his guess for a Reaper. He'd had days to get away instead of continuing the plan that he and his father had crafted to deceive them and take over the organization. They had calculated things meticulously. Everything would've gone as planned, but the Others had kept their focus on the Reapers. Dorcha wasn't even sure the group was real, but he kept giving the Others possibilities for those that could be one of Death's fabled executioners. The fact that Rordan had been a thorn in his side made him an easy target to hand over to the organization.

The look of panic on Fearghal's face when the Fae had brought him into the room had alerted Dorcha that things had gone tits up. His father had said nothing. Then again, there was no need. The defeat was written all over his face. While he looked hale, Dorcha had a feeling his father was anything but.

If he were honest, he had quite enjoyed Fearghal being taken by the Others. It had given Dorcha the time to make his own decisions and do whatever he wanted. He hadn't believed the Others would harm his father after everything their family had done for the group. But he had been wrong. So very wrong. And if he didn't come up with a plan, everything he had worked so hard for would end tonight. He wasn't interested in dying anytime soon.

But the Others weren't all he had to worry about. There was also Rordan.

Dorcha couldn't believe that he hadn't realized Rordan was a Dovecoat. That wasn't the worst part, however. He had seen the look of contempt and determination in Rordan's eyes. He *knew* everything. Dorcha didn't know how Rordan knew the machinations of his operations as well as who his family was, but he did.

Between Rordan and the Others, Dorcha would be lucky to get away with his life. If he managed it, he would be on the run forever.

"Where the fek is Fianna?" he mumbled furiously.

His sister's job was to protect him in just such a scenario. Her absence looked very suspicious. When he found her, he would punish her for not doing her job.

With his ire and dread rising, Dorcha realized that he was trapped. He would either have to face the Others or Rordan. The real threat was the Others. They were the ones who could easily protect him from Rordan. But first, Dorcha needed to convince them that they needed him. With that decision made, he went to their usual meeting location. Just as he expected, his father was there with Hemming. The Light leader of the Others held his father by the arm.

Dorcha walked into the clearing and looked at his da, but Fearghal's gaze was lowered to the ground in defeat.

"Did you figure out you weren't able to get away?" Hemming asked pointedly.

Dorcha jerked his chin to his father. "Let him go. I've given you the Reaper you wanted."

"I find it amusing that you believe that."

Dorcha frowned at the Light. "I have given you more than enough Fae to feed the Others' insatiable need for power. Do you have any idea what it takes to keep the families of those missing from asking too many questions? Perhaps I should just tell the families that those they look for are dead, their magic drained by those of the Others. Not to mention, all those who have joined our cause based on my speeches."

"*Our?*" Hemming asked, brows raised.

"Yes, our," Dorcha snapped, no longer hiding his anger. "My father and I joined the Others long ago, and we worked hard to build the organization to what it is today."

"Dorcha," his father said, a note of warning in his tone.

Dorcha glanced at his father to see him shake his head slightly, a silent plea in his gaze. When Dorcha's eyes slid back to Hemming, the Light was grinning as if he knew something Dorcha didn't. This situation was nothing as Dorcha had expected. Not at all where he'd thought to find himself. "What's going on?"

Fearghal answered. "They found out."

Dorcha's stomach fell to his feet as icy fingers of panic squeezed him. He swallowed, the sound painfully loud, even to him. They had been so careful. There was no way the Others could have discerned anything. But he couldn't say any of that to his father. Not now, at least.

"I don't know what you're referring to," Dorcha finally said.

Hemming released a loud sigh. "By lying, you will only prolong your torment."

Torment? That sounded suspiciously like something that would lead to his death. And if Dorcha feared one thing above anything, it was dying.

Instead of replying to that, he looked around. "Where is Borgar?"

"My colleague is searching for your sister. This is the last time the O'Hannon family attempts a coup. We're wiping you all from existence."

Dorcha began to regret not going with Rordan. Perhaps the two of them could have teamed up and fought the Others. Though, really, it would've just been Rordan. Dorcha knew his weaknesses, and fighting was at the top. He was better at manipulation. Just as he had manipulated his sister all these years.

He shifted his feet as Hemming stared at him dispassionately. His father kept his eyes trained on the ground, leaving Dorcha to deal with…everything. Finally, Borgar arrived. The two leaders traded looks before they turned to Dorcha.

"Where is she?" Borgar demanded.

Dorcha shrugged at the Dark leader. "I've been looking for her since this morning. She's not on the estate."

"She's never far from you," Hemming said. "She's here, and we will find her."

Borgar walked to him, stopping so close that Dorcha had to lean back to keep their bodies from touching. The Dark's red eyes blazed with revulsion. "You disgust me. You've always believed your family was better than anyone else. You had a place with us. But it wasn't enough. You had to reach for more."

"I was following orders," Dorcha hastily said. He detested the coward that he was, but in the end, he had to look out for himself. No one else would.

Borgar clasped his hands behind his back and looked over his shoulder at Hemming. "Isn't that something? Your father said the same thing. Except he told us he was following *your* orders."

Dorcha was so taken aback, he jerked his head to his father. "You bastard."

There was no response from Fearghal.

Borgar chuckled and leaned forward until his nose was all but touching Dorcha's. Then he said in a soft voice, "Two fekking cowards. Neither of you have the balls to admit the truth."

"What do you want? I'll give you anything if you'll allow me to live. I'll serve you however is needed," Dorcha begged.

Borgar's lip lifted in a sneer as he gave him a scathing look. "You can't give us what we're really after."

"What might that be?" Dorcha tried to make his voice stop shaking, but it was impossible since he was quite literally staring death in the face.

"Reapers."

Dorcha blinked at Borgar. "I–I have handed you those I think could be a Reaper."

"You're an imbecile."

"The Reapers are a myth."

Hemming shoved Fearghal onto his knees. "Let's get on with this."

When Borgar reached for him, Dorcha jerked away, lifting his hands in front of him as he did. "Wait. Wait. You wanted powerful families. One of the most powerful is here tonight. Two generations. Renault and Rordan Dovecoat. Everyone knows who the Dovecoats are, even the Dark."

"Having that family in our organization could be beneficial," Hemming said.

To Dorcha's surprise, Borgar dropped his hand and studied him. "Bring them to us, but don't think this will give you much of a reprieve. Your family will pay for your treachery."

"I understand," Dorcha said with a bow of his head.

But all the while, he was planning how he could get himself free. The Others wanted payment because he and his father had attempted to take over the organization. He and his da might have reached a little too high, but in order to succeed, you first had to try. Dorcha realized they may have taken a few too many risks. A mistake he wouldn't make again.

"First," he said in a low voice so his father couldn't hear him, "you should know the truth."

Borgar shot him a bored look. "And what might that be?"

"It wasn't my father who ran things. Or me. It was my sister, Fianna. The fact that she isn't here speaks volumes."

Borgar's red eyes narrowed. "Is that right?"

"I wouldn't lie to you. We were following directions. Fianna is a tyrant. She takes a backseat and gives the appearance of submission, but that isn't the truth. I can bring her to you so you can get the truth out of her."

Borgar motioned Hemming over. The two of them exchanged quiet words before Hemming faced Dorcha with his arms crossed over his chest. "And why should we believe you?"

"Because I want what I've always wanted, to be a part of the Others. I want to see change in the Fae, and I know the Others can do it. My father and I were trapped. He got away from my mother, but he had no idea that Fianna would grow up to be just like her.

She has her eye on a leadership role with the Others, and she won't stop until she gets it. I have no reason to lie to you about this."

Hemming twisted his lips in disgust. "You're turning on your family?"

"Because I'm looking at the bigger picture here," Dorcha said. "The future of the Fae, governed by the Others."

Borgar rolled his eyes. "You and Fearghal blamed each other at first. Why should we believe you now?"

"We fear Fianna. You have no idea who she really is. And if a Fae like my father is terrified of her, that should say something."

The Light and Dark leaders exchanged a look. Dorcha held his breath and kept the smile from showing. He saw his words had swayed them. Once more, his silver tongue would save the day.

"Bring her to us," Borgar stated. "We'll decide what to do with all of you once we hear from her."

"The Dovecoats and the Fae you suspect is a Reaper, as well," Hemming added.

Dorcha licked his lips. "That will be easy enough since he's a Dovecoat."

Borgar slapped him upside the head. "The Reapers are a group, you idiot."

Dorcha wanted to tell them to go find the Reapers themselves, but he bit back the words as he turned on his heel and left to retrieve Fianna. He had no intention of bringing Rordan to the Others. He would watch as Fianna killed him.

CHAPTER TWENTY-ONE

Rordan looked down on the Others and Dorcha from his perch high above them in the trees. He debated moving lower and alerting them that someone was there. But he didn't. He remained where he was, straining to hear their whispered words.

He hadn't caught the last part of their conversation. Though Dorcha's smile made Rordan uneasy. For someone who had been about to die, Dorcha appeared entirely too confident for Rordan's liking. He moved his gaze to Fearghal. On the other hand, the patriarch of the O'Hannon family seemed to have accepted his fate.

Rordan's head snapped to Dorcha when the Fae walked away from the Others. Now Rordan knew for certain that something was up. He wanted to follow Dorcha to see what he was up to, but he didn't want to leave the Others. They were the more important targets. Yet his eyes stayed with Dorcha, his nervous feeling doubling. The only thing that helped was knowing that Fianna was safely away from everything.

Once Dorcha was out of sight, Rordan slid his gaze to the two leaders. They didn't speak, didn't even look at each other. It was apparent by the little he had observed that their relationship was tenuous at best. Would it be fragile enough to break? Rordan was ready to find out. He had wanted more of the Others to show up, but he might as well take what he could get. Two of the group were better than none. The two leaders, even better.

And once Death got a hold of them, they would tell her anything and everything she wanted to know.

"Eoghan," Rordan whispered.

He didn't say more. There was no need. His leader knew what the call meant. Just as he didn't need to tell the Reapers to arrive with their veils raised. Reapers rarely showed up anywhere without their veils in place.

But as the seconds ticked by and he didn't see his fellow brethren, Rordan became concerned. They should have arrived immediately.

Fianna looked toward the east from Rordan's cottage. Moorehall was only a short distance away. She hadn't stopped thinking about what was going on there. The more time that passed without any word from Rordan, the more concerned she became.

And the more she knew she should be there, helping him.

Fianna squeezed her eyes closed. This was the same argument she'd been having with herself for a couple of hours now. Then she would remember that she had promised Rordan she would remain at the cottage. She took her assurances seriously. If she didn't, no one else would. It was her promise that kept getting her hung up about going to check on Rordan.

"He's more than capable of taking care of himself," she said aloud. "He's ten times better than I am, and there wasn't anyone around Dorcha who could come close to besting me."

But Rordan wasn't just facing Dorcha or those in attendance. He was going up against the Others, who, if Rordan was correct in his assessment, were very dangerous. Which had her thinking that she should forget her vow and go help him.

"Bugger it," she ground out as she whirled around and stalked back to the house.

She was halfway there when she heard Dorcha's voice in her head, calling her name. Fianna halted. The part of her that had looked after her brother's safety urged her to answer him, to go to him.

The other part, the bit that had taken the blinders off and had seen her family for the manipulative hypocrites they truly were, had no problem ignoring him.

She continued into the cottage. Inside, she looked around until her gaze landed on the bed. She smiled when she saw it. How she wished she and Rordan were still wrapped in each other's arms on it. For the first time in her life, she knew what it was to be cared for, to be safe, to be…connected to someone on a level she hadn't thought possible.

"Come back to me, Rordan," she said as she wrapped her arms around herself.

A chill suddenly went through her. It was something she had never experienced before. Like the cold hand of death reaching for her. Shaken deeply, Fianna pushed away from the door and looked around for something to busy herself with. She decided on tea and made her way to the kitchen.

"Fek me," Torin mumbled as he picked himself up off the ground.

Cathal blinked and sat up. "You're telling me."

"What the bloody hell happened?" Bradach asked as he held out a hand to Cathal and Aisling to help them to their feet.

Dubhan put his hands on his knees and bent at the waist as he shook his head. "I feel like I've been turned inside out."

Eoghan's head throbbed viciously, and he felt the eyes of his Reapers turn to him for answers. He climbed to his feet and dusted himself off. "It's a barrier, preventing anyone from teleporting inside."

"We're Reapers," Aisling stated.

Balladyn glanced toward Moorehall. "I didn't think anything could keep us out—or in."

"Only one other time has something kept us out," Eoghan said as he stared at the spot before them. He reached out and tentatively moved his hand, only to feel resistance.

"Bran," Cathal murmured with distaste.

Eoghan nodded and looked at Balladyn. "He had syphoned Erith's power, giving him what he needed to keep us out. That means, the Others somehow have that ability, as well."

"Rordan called for us too late," Dubhan said.

Aisling shook her head and wound her long, black and silver hair into a bun at the back of her head. "We have no idea what Rordan was doing. He called for us when he could."

"I agree," Bradach replied.

There was only one thing left for Eoghan to do. "Death."

In the next heartbeat, Erith and Cael arrived, the couple clad in all black, Erith's a mixture of leather and chainmail. Lavender eyes landed on Eoghan as Death quirked a brow.

"The Others are here," he told them.

Cael nodded. "What are you waiting for?"

"We can't get to Rordan or the Others."

Cael's head whipped toward Moorehall as Erith's brow furrowed deeply. She said nothing as she walked to the barrier. As a goddess, she had infinitely more power than the Reapers. She was able to get through, but it wasn't easy for her. Once inside, she turned back to them and met Cael's gaze.

"Go," he told her. "I'm right behind you."

In the next blink, Death was gone. Cael turned to Eoghan. "You know what to do."

Eoghan nodded as Cael followed his mate. To prove that Cael was no longer just a Fae but also a god, he too was able to get through the barrier.

"At least Rordan will have some help," Balladyn said.

Eoghan faced his Reapers. "We're not finished. Spread out and begin attacking the barrier with magic. It will hopefully weaken it enough so that we can get through."

The Reapers hurried to carry out his orders, leaving Eoghan alone. He began to doubt his decision not to have someone with Rordan as backup. If anything happened to Rordan, or any of his Reapers…. He didn't even want to finish the thought. He and Cael knew what it meant to lose Reaper brethren.

It was a blow Eoghan wasn't sure he could handle again. He formed a bubble of magic between his palms, even as his mind drifted to his wife, Thea. She had pulled him from certain death with her haunting violin music. For her, he had returned to this realm. For her, he had opened his heart again.

He might be the leader of a group of Reapers, but she was the one who got him through the difficult times. She stood by him, never wavering in her love. He couldn't wait to get back to her and have her arms around him. With just a hug, she could melt away the horrors of a day. And he had a feeling he would need her desperately when this was finished.

Eoghan reared back his hand and lobbed the orb of magic at the barrier. It slammed against it, sparks flying. Again and again, he threw magic, each strike mightier than the last. Because one of his Reapers was inside.

Because a family member needed help.

Rordan glanced around for any sign of his brethren. His apprehension doubled when they didn't appear. Something was very, very wrong. He glanced at the Others. He wasn't afraid of taking them on himself. He was a Reaper, after all.

Even if fighting them cost him his life, he would gain some

knowledge of the Others. Hopefully, he would stay alive long enough to either pass on that information to the Reapers or give them time to arrive.

Rordan was about to jump to the ground when he spotted someone walking through the forest toward them. It wasn't Dorcha, but something about the person was familiar. He only saw the top of them, and no matter which way he leaned, he couldn't get a view of their face.

"Well, well, well," Borgar said when he spotted the Fae. "Who do we have here?"

Both Hemming and Fearghal looked to see what Borgar meant. It was Hemming who smiled and replied, "Ignore my associate. What can we do for you?"

Their attitude was so different from what it had been with Dorcha that Rordan was taken aback. But it was nothing compared to what he felt when the visitor spoke.

"I've come for you."

Rordan's mouth dropped open. He knew that voice. Xaneth. He started to call for Eoghan again, then decided against it. If Xaneth was here, then the two of them could battle the Others.

Borgar laughed. "Have you now? Then come and get me."

Rordan lowered his veil and leapt from the tree to land beside Xaneth. The royal Fae didn't even look his way.

"Who the fek are you?" Borgar asked.

Rordan smiled. "Someone very interested in you and your friend."

Borgar widened his stance. "What are you waiting for?"

Hemming held out a hand toward Fearghal and formed a ball of magic. Then, without looking at the elder O'Hannon, he pushed it into the back of Fearghal's head. The Fae didn't even have time to give a cry of pain before he was dead. Hemming made his way to Rordan and Xaneth before Fearghal had disintegrated to ash.

Out of the corner of his eye, Rordan watched as Xaneth and Borgar clashed. Rordan focused on Hemming as the Fae pulled back his hands before releasing two orbs of magic. Rordan rolled to the side to dodge them before coming up on one knee and releasing his own blast of magic. He climbed to his feet and threw a ball low. Hemming never saw it as he was too intent on the one coming at his head.

The Light dodged the first orb, but the second hit him on the left shin. It knocked Hemming's foot back, causing him to fall flat on his face. He rolled onto his back and did a kick-up to his feet. As he turned, he sent three quick shots of magic at Rordan.

Rordan weaved to dodge the blasts, though one came entirely too close for comfort. He was more than surprised that the wound on Hemming's leg didn't seem to pain him. The Light hadn't slowed or even limped. Had he not gone down, Rordan would have wondered if he had even struck the Other.

He moved closer to Hemming, alternating throwing magic and his knives. Most Fae only battled with magic, but not him—or any of the Reapers. Getting closer to an opponent meant that it became more difficult to dodge magic for both of them. It was a price Rordan was willing to pay. He landed two more volleys of magic— and three knives. And still, the Light didn't show any signs of stopping.

Rordan winced as one of Hemming's orbs hit his left hip. The magic burned through his clothes and skin into the muscle and cartilage, all the way down to the bone. The pain was excruciating. He ignored it and took the final step as he threw another ball of magic that would bring him close enough for hand-to-hand combat.

He got the chance when Hemming ducked the orb aimed at his face. When he straightened, Rordan punched him in the jaw and did a twisting flip over Hemming to land behind him and then punched him in the kidney. Just as Rordan was getting ready to send a volley of magic, the Light spun away.

They clashed again in a flurry of fists and elbows, each landing several hits. In between punches, balls of magic were thrown until both of them were covered in wounds. Rordan's healed quickly thanks to him being a Reaper. But to his shock, Hemming healed even faster.

Rordan deflected a punch from Hemming, then grabbed Hemming's arm with his left hand and twisted as he smashed his elbow into the Light's face. The crack of bone, followed by a spray of blood, caused Hemming to howl with anger. He used Rordan's move against him and flipped behind Rordan. Before Rordan had a chance to move away, agony radiated from the middle of his back outward. He tried to stay on his feet, to keep fighting, but the magic was already affecting his spine. He fell forward, landing heavily. He gritted his teeth against the stinging pain and rolled onto his side. He got a glimpse of Xaneth and Borgar off to the side. The royal didn't have a single wound on him, while the Dark Other had several.

Hemming came to stand before Rordan, blocking his view of the fight.

"Ready to die?" the Light asked.

Rordan smiled through the agony and the healing of his wound. "I won't be the one dying tonight."

"You're state of lying on the ground in discomfort says otherwise," Hemming stated.

Rordan didn't reply. He was giving his body all the time it needed to heal. He wanted Hemming to think he was dying, that he was weak.

Hemming dropped to one knee and raised an arm up and back as a ball of magic formed. "Only the infamous Reapers could have held their own with us. I thought you would be more of a challenge. I can't wait to tell those in my organization. Now that we know we can best you, we'll wipe you all out in a blink."

Questions flooded Rordan's mind. "You have no idea what you're talking about."

"Oh, but I do," Hemming replied with a smile.

As the Light thrust his hand down to deal a killing blow, Rordan raised his hand with his own bubble of magic and slammed it into the side of Hemming's face. The Light bellowed in pain and rolled away.

Rordan jumped to his feet, ignoring the lingering pain of his wounds. "You're going to tell me everything I want to know."

Hemming held the side of his face, now burned, as he looked up at Rordan. He shook his head, then a frown formed. Rordan grabbed him by the back of the neck, unable to hold back his smile as he pressed the blade of one of his knives against the Fae's throat.

"Did you just try to teleport?" Rordan tsked. "That's not very nice. We aren't finished here."

"You're going to die, Reaper."

Movement out of the corner of his eye caught Rordan's attention. The sight of his father with shock and pride in his eyes caused Rordan to lose his train of thought.

"Is it true?" Renault asked.

Rordan knew what his father was asking, but he couldn't answer. Even if he wanted to.

Renault swallowed, his lips turning up in a smile. "It's all right. You don't need to say. I just wa—"

His father's words were cut off as a blast of magic from Hemming hit him square in the chest. Rordan pulled back his lips in a bellow before his fingers sank into the Light's skin all the way to his spinal column. The moment Rordan felt bone, he yanked out the Other's spine. Hemming disintegrated instantly.

Rordan rushed to Renault as his father dropped to his knees, his hands over his wound. Rordan caught his father as he pitched backward. He glanced at the damage and realized there was nothing that could be done. It was a fatal injury.

"Shite," he ground out helplessly.

Renault shook his head. "It's my fault. I should've remained hidden. I...I gave him a target."

Rordan's throat clogged at the sound of his father's gasping voice. "I should've made sure Hemming couldn't harm anyone else."

"You're a Reaper?" Renault asked, hope filling his eyes.

Rordan knew there would be hell to pay later with Death, but his father was dying. What was the harm? "I died just as my sisters claimed. I've been a Reaper all this time."

"This mi–might mean little now, but I'm proud of you. And I'm so sorry for how things ended with us. I–I should've been a better father."

"Save your breath. You're going to need it," Rordan said.

He was used to death since he reaped souls. But this was different. This was his father slowly dying in his arms. He had hated his family for so long, but none of that mattered now. Maybe it had been his da's apology. Perhaps Rordan had gotten over it long ago. Whatever the reason, the hate no longer resided in him.

Renault lifted a blood-soaked palm. Rordan glanced at it before he clasped it with his fingers.

"My son. You are everything I hoped you would be and more."

Then, with one last smile, his father breathed his last. Rordan's throat clogged with emotion as his vision swam. He stayed until Renault's body began to turn to ash. Only when the last bit drifted through the air did Rordan climb to his feet.

CHAPTER TWENTY-TWO

"Fianna!"

She sighed, wishing she could shut out Dorcha's voice. He sounded frantic. She couldn't help but think that's exactly how he should sound after everything he and their father had done to her.

"It's Rordan. He's hurt. Badly. He told me about the two of you. I really think you should come."

The cup of tea fell from her numb fingers. It crashed onto the wooden floor, startling her. Fianna stared down at the fragments. They looked similar to what her heart would feel like if she lost Rordan.

You promised Rordan you'd remain behind.

But what if he was wounded?

Wouldn't he call for you himself?

"What if he can't?" she asked.

Fianna rose on shaky legs. Promise or not, if someone had injured Rordan , she wanted to be there with him. She could deal with Dorcha later. What mattered was Rordan.

Without a second thought, she jumped to Moorehall, following the sound of her brother's voice.

Rordan turned to help Xaneth because the Reapers needed Borgar. The royal had his back to Rordan as he and the Dark fought. Rordan only got two steps in before Xaneth tore the Dark apart—literally. Shock reverberated through Rordan at the brutality, the savagery of the violence. He stayed where he was, instinct telling him to remain quiet.

Xaneth's shoulders rose as he drew in a deep breath. Then he looked at Rordan, their gazes meeting. Rordan was taken aback at the emptiness he saw within Xaneth's silver depths. The royal Fae looked Rordan up and down and started to walk away.

"Wait, Xaneth," Rordan called.

The Fae halted, turning his head to the side. "You want no part of me."

"I'm a friend. We've been looking for you."

"You would be better to forget you ever knew me."

Rordan knew he had to get Xaneth to stay. "Erith wishes to speak with you."

His brows drew together as he said something under his breath, and then he vanished.

Rordan didn't get a chance to chase him as three Others rushed into the clearing right for him. The three swarmed him, attacking him. He got in several good hits of magic—as well as fists. Then, suddenly, one of the Others went down. Rordan got a glimpse of Aisling before she went after another of the attackers. Within moments, both Others were dead.

"We need one alive," Rordan said, out of breath.

Aisling shrugged a shoulder. "Then we better tell the rest of the gang."

She headed toward the manor as Rordan ran deeper into the forest.

"Where is he?" Fianna asked as she looked around for Rordan.

Dorcha simply stared at her.

Fianna tamped down her rising anger. "Dorcha? Where is Rordan?"

"So, it's true. I took a guess, and it's *true*."

She frowned at the note of hostility in her brother's voice. "What of it? Did you think I wouldn't find out about you and Lewis?"

"Who cares about him? I asked you a question."

"You can go bugger yourself. I don't answer to you or Da any longer."

Dorcha snorted. "Oh, you're going to be answering to someone all right."

"What's that supposed to mean?" She shook her head, unable to believe she'd allowed herself to fall into the trap of fighting with Dorcha like they used to. "Forget it. I don't care. Tell me where Rordan is."

Dorcha merely stared at her as if she were some grotesque thing.

"It was a lie." She should've known. If Rordan had been injured, he would've called for her himself if he wanted her, just like her subconscious had warned. Had she wanted to see him so badly that she would fall for any lie? Apparently.

She couldn't believe she had been so naïve.

"I'm done with you, with Da, with this family. Don't call for me again because I won't come," she told Dorcha.

"You owe us."

Fianna jerked back, surprised at her brother's words. "What?"

"You owe us. *Me.*"

"You're delusional. I'm not going to discuss this anymore."

She turned to leave, but he grabbed her hand, halting her. "Oh, you're going to listen as I remind you of your place."

Rordan had already come upon Cathal, who had taken out the Other he'd been fighting. Now he, Aisling, and Cathal tried to get to the other Reapers to stop them from killing the final Others.

As Rordan rushed through the forest, he spotted motion through the trees. Thinking it might be an Other, he slowed and raised his veil to get closer. Then he heard Fianna's voice. Rordan's blood ran cold.

He jumped to her. He reached for her at the same time he saw Dorcha. Everything moved in slow motion as Fianna kicked her brother, her foot landing in his chest. Dorcha's hold loosened, and he stumbled backward. Fianna tried to teleport out, but Dorcha threw a net at her. The silver net spread wide.

Fianna was quick and spun around, but the webbing tripped up her feet. She fell forward as Rordan lowered his veil, the same instant Dorcha thrust a dagger into Fianna's back.

A roar left Rordan, shattering the slow-motion events. Dorcha's head snapped to him. Without a thought, Rordan withdrew two of his knives and sank them into Dorcha's neck. Then Rordan fell to his knees beside Fianna to gently turn her over and gather her into his arms.

He had already lost his father. He couldn't lose her, too.

"Fi, look at me. That's it, sweetheart. Look at me," he said, forcing a smile he didn't feel when their eyes met.

Her gaze softened, the pain falling away. "Rordan," she whispered.

"Shhh. Everything is going to be fine. Just keep your eyes open. I'm going to take you to someone who can help." Rordan knew it was against the rules, but he didn't care. The Dragon Kings owed the Reapers, and he would call in a favor. Constantine, King of Dragon Kings, could heal anything.

And he would heal Fianna.

Rordan started to gather her tighter to him, ready to jump, when her eyes slid closed. "Fianna? Fi, baby, look at me. Open your eyes. Please, sweetheart. Look at me. Fi? Come on. You're strong. You can get through this. Just open your eyes."

When he saw the first movement of ash, he was unable to move, unable to think. Someone grabbed him from behind, and the next thing Rordan knew, he was somewhere else. And Fianna was gone.

He threw back his head and let out a bellow of rage, agony... and loss.

Rordan fought like a wild thing to get away, using magic and physical strength. He lashed out, hitting whoever he could, all the while roaring Fianna's name over and over again.

Eoghan held him, refusing to let go. But he wasn't the only one. Every Reaper was there, keeping Rordan from returning to Fianna. The last thing Rordan needed was to see someone he loved disintegrate. Eoghan's heart hurt for Rordan, because he knew just how devastating the loss would be. And the ripples it would cause would be felt for many centuries to come.

That was if Rordan survived.

CHAPTER TWENTY-THREE

The pain subsided. Fianna breathed a sigh of relief even as her heart clutched, recalling Rordan's voice breaking as he called her name. A tear escaped from between her lids. She didn't want to open her eyes because the world she had known, the one Rordan had been in, was gone. The Fae never spoke much of the afterlife. The majority assumed that once they were reduced to ash, they were simply no more.

Now she knew that wasn't the truth. She had her consciousness, at least. And if she opened her eyes, she might find out more. Yet, she couldn't. Cowardice kept her eyes tightly shut, and her mind full of thoughts of Rordan.

She heard a sigh from someone near. "It would be easier if you opened your eyes."

Fianna hadn't expected a feminine voice. She hadn't expected anyone. Curious, she lifted her lids and found herself looking at the same trees she had seen before she died. She turned her head to discover a beautiful female sitting on the ground, her knees drawn up to her chest. She noted she wore armor, which Fianna approved of. The leather breastplate had a Celtic design on it that matched the arm vambraces. The outfit's skirt was leather strips and chainmail that reminded her of something the Roman army wore or....

"Xena," Fianna said.

The warrior quirked one finely arched black brow. "Excuse me?"

Fianna shook her head, unable to believe she had said the name aloud. She glanced around for a sign of Rordan. "Your outfit reminds me of Xena, the Warrior Princess."

"He isn't here."

Her head snapped back to the female. "How do you know who I was looking for?"

The warrior smiled softly, her lavender eyes crinkling at the corners. She tossed her long, blue-black locks over her shoulder and placed her forearms on her knees. "Because I know who you are."

"And who are you?"

"I've gone by several names. Mistress of War is one. Death is another."

Fianna was so shocked that she couldn't form words.

Death blew out a breath and shifted so that she sat facing Fianna. "I hold your soul, preventing your death. For the moment."

"I see." Though she really didn't. But what did one say to…Death?

Death tilted her head to the side, causing a wave of hair to fall over one shoulder. "Fae warriors have always caught my attention. The best keep it. You, Fianna, are exceptional. And it's those extraordinary warriors, those who have been betrayed and murdered, that I make my offer to. As Death, I am judge and jury to the Fae. I have a group known as Reapers, who carry out my judgements. I would like you to join them."

Fianna swallowed, unable to believe that the Reapers were real. The group was hotly debated among the Fae. Then her mind halted. She had been betrayed. And she had been murdered—by her brother.

"Before you decide," Death continued, "there are rules. The first is that no one can know who or what you are. You will lie at all costs to prevent any Fae from learning you're a Reaper. The second is that you obey my every command without hesitation or question."

"Is that all?" Fianna asked as a wave of pain ran through her.

Death shook her head. "You can't have contact with anyone from your past. Not family, friends, lovers. Anyone."

Fianna thought of Rordan. Could she continue living without him?

"As a Reaper, I will give you a second chance. You will have more power, more strength than the average Fae. Your duties, however, will exceed those of just reaping. We fight alongside our allies like the Dragon Kings to protect ourselves and this realm from enemies."

"The Others," she said, thinking of what Rordan had told her of the group.

Death's lips curved into a smile. "Exactly. This second chance doesn't mean you're immortal. You can be killed, but your extra magic will help prevent that, for the most part."

Fianna found all of it intriguing, but her mind had returned to the one who had taken her life. "What of Dorcha? Can I take my revenge on him?"

"He is no more."

Emotion overtook her because Fianna didn't need to ask to know that Rordan had killed him. She should be saddened that her brother was dead, but it was hard to feel anything but relief for the person who had taken her life.

"Your time is running out," Death said. "What is your answer?"

All her life, Fianna had known she was meant to do something great. She'd thought it had been helping her brother and father.

Maybe this was her destiny. She wasn't afraid of dying. She was afraid of losing Rordan, but it appeared that would happen either way. At least with Death's offer, she could make a difference in the world.

"I accept," Fianna said.

Death reached over and touched her with one finger. In an instant, the pain was gone, and she was able to move her legs. Fianna sat up, renewed. There was a smile on her face, even though her heart broke at finally finding love and then having it slip through her fingers.

"Are you ready to meet the rest?"

Fianna got to her feet and used magic to conjure new clothing in all black, but this time more body-hugging. She was shocked to see that Death was shorter than she. "I've never known a Fae with eyes your color."

"That's because I'm not Fae. I'm a goddess."

The words had barely registered before Death grabbed her arm and teleported them to a tiny isle in the middle of a body of water. Death released her and walked through a Fae doorway. Fianna hurried to follow.

"I don't understand. If you aren't Fae, then why can you use our doorways? Why—?"

The questions stopped when Fianna realized they had walked into another realm. The sheer scope of flowers that surrounded the doorway was mesmerizing. The trees stood tall, their limbs stretching wide to create a stunning canopy of interwoven branches. The cacophony of birds singing should have been distracting, but instead, it soothed Fianna.

Animals were everywhere. Some in the distance, some on the limbs above her. The buzzing of bees added to the melody. Fianna could have explored the small area for a lifetime, but she soon realized that Death was walking ahead of her. Fianna quickly caught up with the petite goddess as they wove through the maze of flora and fauna. Through it all, she caught a glimpse of the gleaming white tower.

"For many long millennia, this realm was mine alone. It was my escape. Recently, however, I opened it up to the Reapers to keep us all safe and separate. All live here. The realm is large enough that you can find a place that suits you."

Fianna halted with Death when they emerged from the garden. They stared at the tower for a moment. The one thing she noticed was how quiet it was. There was no hum of cars, no noise of people. Fianna never wanted to leave.

Movement at the base of the tower drew her attention. Fianna spotted a male, though his gaze was locked on Death. And the smile he gave her made Fianna long to see Rordan.

"This is my mate, Cael," Death said. "He's also the leader of one group of my Reapers."

Fianna perked up. So, Reapers could find love. There was still a chance for Rordan, because she knew he was an exceptional warrior. Then her hope faded as she realized that Rordan would have to be betrayed and killed to be offered the chance. She couldn't imagine that happening to him.

Cael reached them. He bowed his head of black hair, but it wasn't silver eyes Fianna saw. They were purple. "You chose wisely," he said.

"Thank you," Fianna replied, unable to look away from his face.

Cael chuckled as he wrapped an arm around Death. "You're wondering about my eyes?"

"I apologize for staring, but they're as unusual as Death's."

"Call me Erith," Death said. "It's the name I go by with the Reapers."

Fianna bowed her head. "Erith."

Cael drew in a breath and glanced at his mate. "I didn't always have these eyes. This is a recent change. We were battling an enemy, who tried to use Erith's magic against me. It backfired. I became something...more."

"A god," Erith chimed in.

Fianna's eyes widened even as Cael gazed at his mate with such devotion that she felt her heart break, knowing she would most likely never experience such a thing again. She'd had it briefly with Rordan, and she would have to be content with that.

"When we become Reapers, we cease being just Fae, even though we retain the coloring we had in life," Cael continued. "Those here are not Light or Dark. They are Reapers. We are, in fact, a family."

Fianna nodded, listening through the heartache that had suddenly come over her.

"I think it's time she met some of the others," Erith said.

Suddenly, another male stood before her. He had long, black hair and molten silver eyes. He bent slightly at the waist. "I'm Eoghan, another leader of the Reapers. Why don't I show you around and introduce you to the others?"

Fianna forced a smile that she didn't feel. She was overwhelmed by everything and wanted some time to herself, but that didn't look like it would happen anytime soon. With no other choice, she followed Eoghan away from Cael and Erith.

"All of this is a shock, I know. You'll get the hang of it quickly, though," he said.

"I hope so."

Eoghan halted and looked at her. "I think I'll wait to introduce you to everyone. I would like to show you a spot I think will help with everything. Then, I'll leave you and let you explore on your own."

"That would be nice," she told him.

Eoghan held out his arm. The moment she touched it, they were transported to the top of a cliff with a vast ocean before her. Fianna immediately thought of how similar it looked to Rordan's cottage on Achill.

"You might look over there," Eoghan said as he pointed to the left.

She followed his gaze and found a male form standing on the outcropping of a cliff. Even with his silhouette, she knew him instantly. Her heart leapt in excitement. She forgot all about Eoghan and started running toward Rordan with tears streaming down her face.

Fianna slowed to a walk when she got close. For several moments, she could only stare at the back of him, too overcome with emotion. She took another tentative step and whispered his name. When he turned, she was taken aback by the haunted face that greeted her. It transformed instantly when he saw her.

"Fi," he said and dragged her against his body, holding her so tightly she could barely breathe.

But she didn't care. All she had wanted was to feel his arms again, and now she was. She relished every second they shared, each basking in the disbelief and wonder of the moment.

Rordan pulled back, holding her at arm's length. "How?"

"I'm a Reaper," she said with a smile.

He threw back his head and laughed. "I should've known. I wanted to tell you all of it."

"I know, and I understand why you couldn't. But that means… you died."

"I did. My family betrayed me."

"I'm sorry."

"I'm sorry it happened to you, as well." Rordan gently touched her face. "I thought I had lost you."

"I'm here now."

Rordan nodded, smiling.

Fianna drew in a breath and blurted out the words she had been holding inside her. "I love you."

He smiled and lowered his forehead to hers. "I never thought I'd hear those words from your lips. Say them again."

"I love you. I love you now and forever. You see me. You accept all of me as no one ever has. I feel safe and loved with you."

Rordan raised his head and cupped her face with his hands. "You have my heart. You have all of me from this day forward until the end of time. I love you as I never thought I could love someone. You are…everything to me."

He covered her mouth with his as they gave in to the sizzling kiss.

❧

Cael lifted Erith's hand to his lips, their fingers entwined, as they watched the couple embrace. "You could've told Rordan what you'd planned."

"And what if she had said no? I couldn't do that to him," she said.

"We would've lost him. He wouldn't have survived without her."

Erith sighed and turned her head to meet his gaze. "That isn't why I offered Fianna the position. She earned it, and she will make an excellent Reaper. It's fortunate that things worked out as they did."

"Love is more powerful than any type of magic," Cael said as he swung his attention back to the couple.

Erith wound her arms around him and leaned into his side. "It saved you, my love. And it saved me."

They smiled at each other before jumping back to their tower.

EPILOGUE

The next day…

Rordan couldn't stop smiling. His world had come to an end the day before, only to be resuscitated by Fianna's arrival. He didn't know when Erith had decided that Fianna would be a Reaper, and it didn't matter. None of the past did anymore.

There had been no sleep during the night as he and Fianna talked and made love and talked some more. She was disappointed at not being able to search out and speak to her mother now that she was a Reaper, but she could at least see her from afar. It was something Rordan would make sure Fianna got to do soon. That was part of the plans they had made during the long hours of the night.

He watched as Fianna was introduced to the rest of the Reapers. When it came time to meet Balladyn, she had been speechless, but the former King of the Dark had bowed his head and welcomed her into the fold. It was rare for a new Reaper to be created, and they'd had two in quick succession.

When Rordan spotted Cael and Erith off to the side, he made his way to them. "In my…turmoil…yesterday, I never asked if any of the Others had been captured."

"Unfortunately, they learned what we were trying to do and retreated before we could secure one," Erith explained.

That meant their hunt for the Others was still on. "They know of us. They intend to wipe us out."

Cael snorted. "Do they now?"

Rordan exchanged a grin with Cael because they were both eager to face the Others again. Rordan turned his attention back to Erith. "I do have some news you might like. I saw Xaneth."

Erith went still. "What?"

"He was there?" Cael asked with a frown.

Rordan nodded. "He walked out as I called for Eoghan to fight the Others. Xaneth would've faced both the leaders on his own, but I lowered my veil and joined him. When the battle was over, I tried to get him to wait, but he said it was better if he didn't. Then he was gone."

"Did he say anything else?" Erith asked in a soft voice.

"He simply told me that it would be better if we forgot we ever knew him."

Cael blew out a breath. "Should we do as he asks?"

"No," Erith stated before she walked away.

A moment later, Cael followed. Rordan returned to Fianna's side as she and Aisling shared a smile over something Cathal had said. Rordan watched as his brethren stood together, those with mates, and those without. Their family was growing, which made him smile.

Then he recalled Hemming's words about the Others' plan for the Reapers.

～

Torin shifted his shoulders. Ever since he had gotten that feeling about Rordan being in trouble, he couldn't shake it. It was like a dark cloud hanging over him—over all of them. And he knew it had to do with the Others.

It didn't help that the Others had put a target on the Reapers' backs. Time was running out. He wasn't sure for who, but he knew the clock was ticking.

～

The calm that had descended over Xaneth after killing the evil on Achill Island hadn't lasted long. Once more, he could smell the stench of malevolence permeating everything, everywhere. All he wanted was to sleep, to rest without the nightmare within pulling him back under.

But that couldn't happen until all the wickedness was gone for good.

Thank you for reading
DARK ALPHA'S OBSESSION.
Want to know what happens
next in the Dark World?
Order **DRAGON MINE** right now at
www.DonnaGrant.com!

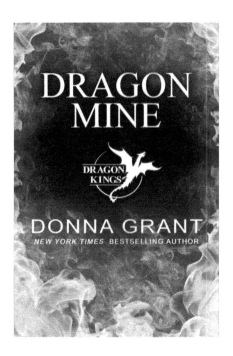

From *New York Times* and *USA Today* bestselling author
Donna Grant comes a new story in her
Dragon Kings series...

**Order DRAGON MINE
in print, ebook, and/or audio today!**

Donna Grant
www.DonnaGrant.com
www.MotherofDragonsBooks.com

EXCERPT OF DRAGON MINE

DRAGON KINGS SERIES, BOOK 2

Dreagan
February

"Vaughn."

He turned toward seductive voice, seeking the supple body, the pleasure he knew awaited. His arms wound about her as his lips descended upon hers. The kiss was fire and flame, consuming and devouring. They were skin to skin, their limbs tangled as they sought to get closer, ever closer.

The passion had begun as a spark the instant his eyes had landed upon her. That spark soon turned into an inferno. The intensity of what he felt, the force of his need, his *hunger*, left him shaking.

And the only cure was her.

He groaned when her hand slipped between them and wrapped around his arousal. She moved her hand up and down his length, pulling him closer and closer to an orgasm. He didn't know how many times they had shared their bodies. Whenever he was with her, time ceased. There was nothing but her.

His breathing hitched. He wanted to stop her, to wait to have his pleasure until he'd made her climax at least twice. Her lips traveled down his neck and lower to his chest. Her mouth wrapped around his nipple and she flicked her tongue over it. He was powerless to resist her. Wherever she touched, he *burned*. Eager for more.

With every pump of her hand, he felt his orgasm approaching. He tried to open his eyes and see her face, but he couldn't. Then it didn't matter because his body was flooded with ecstasy. He reached for her, needing to hold her to feel her against him. Only she was gone.

Vaughn wrenched open his eyes to find himself alone, his harsh breaths filling the room. He glanced down at his stomach to see the evidence of his dream.

"Fuck," he murmured and rolled out of bed to clean himself off.

He tossed aside the towel and stood in the doorway of the bathroom looking at his bed. The sheets were in disarray, the pillows on the floor. If he didn't know better, he'd say he had a fun romp with someone. Only, there hadn't been anyone but *her*.

When was this going to end? Vaughn wasn't sure how much more he could take. It had been thousands of years since she had come into his life. One night. One beautiful, incredible night. And she vanished like smoke. No matter how far and wide he looked, he had yet to find her. He didn't even know her name.

Hell, he barely remembered her face.

Vaughn shook his head as he dropped his chin to his chest. He could recall every detail of her body. He knew her sighs, her soft moans of pleasure. He knew the smell of her skin, the feel of her against him.

It was the other details he couldn't remember that made him want to bellow to the heavens. When he'd first seen her through the throng of people, it had been instant attraction. The fires had burned all around the village. He hadn't meant to stop, but something had drawn him to the humans.

They had been celebrating a great victory against an enemy. And no one celebrated like the Celts. They welcomed him, shoving a horn of mead into his hand as they danced and sang. Vaughn had always had a particular interest in the Celts. They were attuned to the earth in a way that others weren't.

Vaughn had moved away from the group and leaned against an ancient, gnarled oak with limbs that twisted and reached far to the side. He watched the festivities with a smile. The mead was particularly good. Or perhaps, it was the magic in the air that night.

The British Isle thrummed with magic. It's why the Dragon Kings had made their home in Scotland, the heart of all magic on the planet. Dragon Kings were specially tuned to magic in all beings and creatures. Many times, mortals had no idea that magic was there, sometimes even changing events. That was because the humans couldn't feel it. But Vaughn did. It was thick, hanging heavy in the air like an invisible mist. Even if he had wanted to walk away, he wouldn't have been able to.

Then, across one of the great fires, he saw her. She had stood staring at him. That's when he realized she was the reason he was there. They said nothing as they started toward each other, weaving through others and around fires.

The minute they came face to face, she took his hand and led him to a cottage. The red orange of a fire covered the inside of the home. She faced him, and before he could speak, her mouth was on his. Just thinking about that first kiss made Vaughn groan with longing. Everything he'd ever felt, ever would feel had been in her kiss.

The emotions had been overwhelming at first. But it didn't take long for them to consume him. Just as his desire did.

As it still did, centuries later.

He forgot about hiding who he was from the mortals, forgot about not showing magic in front of them—because he had needed to feel her skin against his. Without hesitation, he had used magic to remove their clothes.

Vaughn had no idea how many times they shared their bodies that night. He'd never had passion take control of him in such a way before. It wasn't until the sun woke him and he found himself alone that he realized he didn't know her name. He hadn't been too worried, at first. He assumed the cottage was hers.

But as hours passed and she didn't return, he decided to go looking for her. No one in the village knew of who he spoke. He hadn't given up, though. He spent over a week with that Celtic tribe hoping to see her again. With each day that passed without her, Vaughn began to wonder if she had been real at all.

He returned to Dreagan and tried to forget that night and her. But it was impossible. That's when his search began. He looked far and wide, combing through the smallest of villages to the biggest cities to no avail. Even when he realized that she was most likely dead, he still looked. Hoping against hope that he would somehow find her one day.

Perhaps that's why he found her in his dreams.

Vaughn blew out a breath and lifted his head. He couldn't go on like this much longer. He didn't know if this unknown woman he'd searched for through thousands of years was his mate or not. Maybe not knowing who she was caused him to latch onto her and dream about her.

Order DRAGON MINE
in print, ebook, and/or audio today!

Donna Grant
www.DonnaGrant.com
www.MotherofDragonsBooks.com

NEVER MISS A NEW BOOK
FROM DONNA GRANT!

Sign up for Donna's newsletter at
http://www.tinyurl.com/DonnaGrantNews

Be the first to get notified of new releases and be eligible for special subscribers-only exclusive content and giveaways. Sign up today!

ABOUT THE AUTHOR

New York Times and *USA Today* bestselling author Donna Grant has been praised for her "totally addictive" and "unique and sensual" stories. She's written more than one hundred novels spanning multiple genres of romance including the bestselling Dark King series that features a thrilling combination of Dragon Kings, Druids, Fae, and immortal Highlanders who are dark, dangerous, and irresistible. She lives in Texas with her dog and a cat.

www.DonnaGrant.com
www.MotherofDragonsBooks.com

facebook.com/AuthorDonnaGrant

instagram.com/dgauthor

bookbub.com/authors/donna-grant

goodreads.com/donna_grant

pinterest.com/donnagrant1

CPSIA information can be obtained
at www.ICGtesting.com
Printed in the USA
LVHW022124270521
688690LV00012B/1380